MW00489679

DALE C. PHILLIPS

based on a screenplay by
Jonathan Levine

BOOKS

REVOLVER BOOKS

Published by Revolver Books

Revolver Entertainment LLC, 8306 Wilshire Blvd #107,
Beverly Hills, CA 90211

First published in the United States of America in 2008 by Revolver Books
an imprint of Revolver Entertainment LLC

ISBN-13: 978-1-905978-14-4
ISBN-10: 1-905978-14-6

Text design and typesetting by Dexter Haven Associates Ltd, London
Printed in the United States of America
Distributed by Publishers Group West

www.revolverbooks.com

one

"I don't get to lie on the couch or nothin'?"

"Would you like to lie on the couch?"

"Is that a trick question?"

"Why would you think that?"

"No reason...I'll stay right here."

But still the couch drew Luke's attention. He pushed his visor to one side to get a better look at it. Lots of people *did* come here and lie on that couch. Luke was sure of it. He could see how the couch had been obsessively, neurotically, psychotically polished by the backs of hundreds of Doctor Squires's patients, leaving an almost perfectly formed body shape on the otherwise dull brown leather like the chalk outline of a murdered corpse.

"It's probably still warm anyway," Luke said.

Doctor Squires looked at him.

"The couch," Luke said. "It's probably still warm from your last patient, isn't it?"

"This isn't a monogamous relationship, Luke. I do have other patients."

"But why *do* people lie on couches in psychiatrists' offices?"

"Why do you think they do it?"

Luke shrugged. "Cuz it's more relaxing lyin' down?"

"It's so they can look at the ceiling. It's the most uncluttered part of the room. Otherwise, they're looking at the clock, or the certificates on the wall, or the artful and pretentious paintings – they came with the office, by the way."

"The certificates?"

"The paintings, Luke."

Luke flipped the visor back over his eyes.

"What's on your mind, Luke?"

Doctor Squires's antique clock shamelessly proclaimed the seconds that passed between them like a table tennis ball...Finally, the rally ended.

"Nothing," Luke replied.

"Well, in that case..."

Doctor Squires pushed his chair back from under the mahogany desk and was about to stand.

"I mean, I guess I can make something up," Luke quickly added.

"Fine. Make something up, then."

"Okay. Let's see...Hmm..."

Luke bit his bottom lip, and his eyes flitted around the ceiling as if searching for inspiration. There was nothing there.

"Are you sure you don't want to lie on the couch, Luke?" Doctor Squires asked. "Or perhaps I could tap the fingertips of one hand against the fingertips of the other, you know, the way you think psychiatrists do? Or how about if I ask my receptionist to go out and get me a bow tie? Do you think that would help?"

Luke looked at Doctor Squires and imagined how ridiculous he would look in a bow tie. He sort of looked ridiculous anyway – in a *VH1* kind of way – what with the graying shoulder length hair, the untidy little goatee. Not that there was anything wrong with a retro seventies look, Luke thought, but unless you're going to also buy vintage clothes, it can look like you've got your head stuck in the past, like a child gets stuck in the railings.

"Well?" Doctor Squires asked.

"Okay. Let's see, I'm having trouble…"

"Yes?"

"I'm having trouble… getting laid."

Doctor Squires looked at him quizzically. "Are you still making this up? Never mind. It's a common problem. How old are you again, Luke?"

"Old enough to be getting laid. And getting older every day."

"Have you ever gotten laid?"

"Two years ago I fucked Katie Randall in Battery Park, but she had drunk two forty ounce bottles and the cops came and broke us up before we – before I – could...Looking back, it was probably a mistake doing it against one of the statues, but who wants to lie down when it's wet?"

"So she was drunk?"

"She weighs, like, sixty pounds and she drank two forty ounce bottles of Crazy Horse. You do the math."

"Crazy Horse?"

"It's a malt liquor. It's got an American Indian on the label."

"Any good?"

"Well, Katie Randall obviously thought so...Doctor Squires, why is that the only thing you've written down?"

Doctor Squires put down his pen.

"Look, Doctor Squires..." Luke said.

"Call me Jeff."

"Look, Jeff – Doctor Squires – how much do you need?"

Doctor Squires sat back in his chair and raised an eyebrow. "You're the one who needs this, son."

"How much, Doctor Squires?"

"A quarter."

Luke dug into his backpack, and pulled out some bags of weed.

"I can give you two eighths. It's the same."

"I can do the math, Luke."

Luke held onto two baggies and put the rest back.

"Here you go, Doctor Squires."

Doctor Squires took the plastic bags and holding each one between a thumb and index finger – like they were meditation bells – he gently moved his fingertips in a circular motion; contrasting the outer smoothness of the synthetic bags with the subtle crunch of their natural contents... Only the sound of Luke zipping up his backpack – like a needle scratching across a record – brought him abruptly back from his sensuous reverie. He blinked. "Okay, Luke, that entitles you to another..." He squinted at his watch, wondering when it was that he'd begun to move his wrist *away* from his face in order to see the time better.

"Another forty-eight minutes," Luke said, glancing at the clock over Doctor Squires's shoulder.

"That's right. Forty-eight minutes. If you leave now you're getting ripped off... And I don't know what the American Board of Psychiatry and Neurology would say if they knew I was ripping off my patients."

Luke stared at him for a second, unsure whether he was serious or not.

"Look, Doctor Squires, I'm really not in the mood to be analyzed today; have my life put under a magnifying glass. It's too fuckin' hot. I'd pop like an ant. Besides, I'm not really feeling all this 'feeling shit' today, anyway."

Luke picked up his backpack and turned to leave.

Doctor Squires stopped him. "Luke, tomorrow's a very big day in your life. One of the biggest. And I look at you – and it looks like you'll mark the day with no more joy than a prisoner counting his sentence making a diagonal line on the wall of his cell. You know?"

Of course Luke knew. But seeing as they both knew, there seemed little point in saying it.

"Tell Stephanie I say whassup. And tell her she owes me."

"Uh-huh," Doctor Squires said, as he pulled out a bong from the drawer of his table.

Luke stopped as he walked past him, and studied his face. He wondered whether this was why the goatee was so frayed – because he couldn't bear to look at himself in the mirror long enough to tidy it.

"You ever feel kinda like a fuck-up, you know?" Luke asked him. "Buying weed from the same guy who deals to your daughter?"

Doctor Squires took a big bong hit, exhaling into a paper towel roll to disguise the smell before his next appointment.

"Stepdaughter," Doctor Squires corrected him.

Jesus! Luke thought. What sort of advice was the next poor fucker going to get?

"Stepdaughter. Exactly…Later, Mr Squires."

Doctor Squires replied with an almost desperate urgency: "I'm a Doctor, Luke! I'm a Doctor!"

Luke smiled and nodded to himself as he opened the door. "Doctor Squires."

But momentarily, this seemed to be less of a reminder for Luke; Doctor Squires pulled his mouth away from the bong before he inhaled.

"Has it been no help at all coming here today, son?"

Luke pulled his backpack onto his shoulders. "Well, my bag's a quarter of an ounce lighter."

two

As Luke sat in the subway car on his way home, bobbing his head to "The World is Yours" by Nas in his headphones, he wondered what exactly Doctor Squires had wanted to hear about his life. He rehearsed it in his head.

"Once upon a time – 1994 to be exact – on an island called Manhattan, lived a kid named me, Luke Shapiro. Seventeen years of age – and getting older every day…"

Fuck! This was stupid! Luke decided. Average weight. Average height. No distinguishing features. Aside from the fact he sold weed, there was nothing much remarkable about him. And even the drug thing was just a cry for help, really.

My name is Luke Shapiro. I am a drug dealer. Hear me cry.

He tried to think about the things he liked. Was there anything remarkable there? He liked the summer. But maybe not for the same reasons that everyone else did. Luke liked it in the summer when

the air smelled of sunshine and cigarettes; he liked the summer storms (they were so much louder and more violent than the winter storms, because the trees were so full and heavy); and when the city warmed up, like a turd on a radiator, he liked the summer stench in the subway.

Luke closed his eyes, opened up his lungs and took a deep toke. (One to remember for when the summer was over.) Yup. That's the one. *One hundred percent summer subway stench.*

And he liked alliteration. He learned about that in English class. "Alliteration," the English teacher informed them, "was one of language's musical instruments, which was why it was often to be found in poetry..." And every other wack headline and crappy advertising slogan. But it was also in every other comic book (Peter Parker, Clark Kent, Green Goblin, Lex Luthor, Lois Lane), and Luke liked that. He remembered also being taught about assonance – the repetition of vowel sounds – to be found within an expression like "The lazy days of summer." Luke wasn't quite so keen on assonance. It was harder to spot.

"*The laaazy daays of summer.*"
"*The laaazy daays of summer.*"
"*The laaazy daays of summer.*"

Luke suddenly realized he wasn't saying these words in his head.

She glanced away as soon as he caught her looking at him, but not in that embarrassed cute way – it was one of those disgusted sideways glances which normally begin their journeys with a slow blink and a sharp "tut." Luke didn't mind. High school had gotten him used to this look. But fuck! She was beautiful. The dark hair. High cheekbones. Great tits. She reminded Luke of Fran Drescher from that fucking awful show that came out last year, *The Nanny*. (Luke used to watch it with the sound down.) And she reminded Luke of something else that he liked: seeing sweaty girls on the train in short skirts – and seeing their panties, whenever he got the chance.

There were, however, ways of improving his chances.

Normally Luke would slouch back in his seat (to improve his line of sight), pulling his visor down to just above his eye line (to disguise his intentions).

But, then again, she'd already made the assumption that he was a subway lunatic, so what the fuck did he have to lose?

He leant forward to cop a sneaky look. And she instinctively preserved her modesty by crossing her legs, but in doing so, for a split second, Luke was sure he glimpsed white panties, bordered by jet-black pubic hair on either side of the gusset. Or maybe it was just a shadow.

Luke sat back again. He could see his reflection, partly obscured by her body, in the dark train window

opposite. The aisle had vanished. He was behind her now. He imagined fucking her doggie style – her big fleshy tits oozing from between the fingers of each of his hands. The train shook. So did the image. Violent thrusts as he quickly found his rhythm, aided by a pussy already half-lubricated by the summer. *Have some of that, you super-hot fuckin' Nanny bitch. And that! And that! And that!*

Yes. Luke liked fly ladies. He liked tank tops. He liked short skirts. And he especially liked his impure thoughts... Was this what Doctor Squires had wanted to hear about?

Luke imagined a subway car full of fly girls – blondes, brunettes, redheads – but all wearing the same tight, white tank top and a skirt so short, they'd have to wax to wear it.

"Do you know what I'd do to them, Doctor Squires? Well, first I'd roll them a big blunt, and they would be very impressed – no one empties a cigar and fills it with dope like I do – my blunt-rolling skills are, in a word, mad impressive. Then I'd put on some music..."

Luke imagined pulling out the headphones from his walkman – and, fantastically, music filled the subway car as Luke walked through it.

"And they'd start to move their heads, Doctor Squires, like every beat of the music was an invisible cock – and they just *had* to suck it. And then they'd start to move their long fuckin' legs, making their skirts ride up even higher on their thighs, pushing their panties up between their legs. And now, they leap up from their seats cuz they're filled with a sensation – a seriously sinful sexual sensation that makes 'em drip inside. They're riding the subway poles, dancing with each other, rubbing their bodies together. And you know that smell I like, Doctor Squires, the summer subway stench? Well, it just got better, it just got cut with quim. That subway car is one long tube of vagina – vagina that's thinking of one thing, and one thing only: *Sha-pir-o! Sha-pir-o! Sha-pir-o!*"

The fantasy abruptly ended on 42nd Street when the subway doors dinged open and a million businessmen in suits piled into the subway train.

Luke shook his head. Cunts.

Luke knew it was only a matter of time before Doctor Squires – in trying to find the root of the problems that so filled Luke's head that they threatened to squeeze from every orifice like Play-Doh – asked him about his childhood...

And the truth was, Luke had experienced a very traumatic childhood indeed: his parents had stayed married.

Luke kept his headphones on as he walked from the street and into the family apartment. After all, he didn't need to hear the argument to know what his

parents were warring about. It was always the same
thing all wars were about.

Money.

And as usual, they were arguing in the hallway.
("The reason for this, Doctor Squires, is that the old
woman who lives in the apartment on the other side of
the hallway, she's got a hearing problem. Whereas the
family who lives in the apartment on the other side of
the front room, well, they just got a new car.")

Luke walked obliviously between the pointing
fingers and the spittle as they faced off in the narrow
space. (He felt like a punk rock act.) His parents never
acknowledged him either. It was like he was a ghost,
haunting them from a time gone by, when – by the fact
of his very existence – they must have got on better
than they did now.

"I guess they were in love once, Doctor Squires, I
just can't figure out how. But although I've heard it
said that family teaches us the most important lesson in
life – how to get along with people we don't like –
what's strange is, one-on-one, I like them just fine. And
I know it's cool to say you don't like your folks, but,
honestly, I really don't mind 'em. What I *do* mind is
them yelling at each other 24/7. That I fucking mind a
lot… The thing is, parents have an only child for
various reasons, but more often than not, it's because
they think they'll find it easier – but the kid's still gotta
deal with two fuckin' parents. Alone."

Luke climbed the stairs that led to his bedroom like he was climbing a mountain – moving from left to right, sometimes pulling himself up three steps at a time – trying to avoid the cardboard boxes that were scattered all over them. (In fact, they were scattered all over the small apartment.)

"Dad's a true businessman, Doctor Squires, an entrepreneur and shit, which sucks cuz he has to wear a suit, but which is cool for him – I guess – because he feels successful. All the fucking cardboard boxes are his. He hasn't told us what they are yet, but merely refers to it as 'Project X,' which makes it sound mysterious and exciting…and conveniently hides the fact that 'Projects A–W' had been woeful failures."

Eventually, Luke made it to his bedroom, closed the door and gave it the finger. He threw off his visor, took off his headphones, and pulled his sticky T-shirt over his head. He could do with a shower, but he couldn't bear to go out there again. So he splashed some Nautica cologne under his arms and put on a new T-shirt.

And he stuck his headphones back on.

"You see, Dad doesn't make much money these days, Doctor Squires, but he's a workaholic just the same. I hardly see the guy, which is alright by me. But even when I do see him, he mostly stays out of my business."

Luke opened a mini-fridge and pulled out a big brick of weed.

"I think he might even know I'm dealing, but he's never tried to bother me about it... But then again, why should he? It's the nineties. Dealing weed isn't exactly a capital offense."

An hour and a half later, the argument had blown itself out. Luke liked to give it at least another half an hour to be on the safe side, but hunger forced him to leave his bedroom and make for the kitchen.

He opened the fridge door. It was barely worth the light coming on.

"Are you hungry, Luke? Do you want me to make something for you?"

Luke looked behind him. It was his mom sitting at the dinner table.

"Why are you sitting in the dark, Mom?"

"Oh, I got a headache."

"Hmm... and why do you think that is? Do you think it might have something to do with all the shouting and screaming?"

She didn't say anything, but Luke could see from the light that shone from the open fridge that she'd closed her eyes and was squeezing her temples with her fingers.

"Are you okay?" he asked her. "Do you want me to get you anything?"

"I'm okay. I'll be okay. Did you want me to make you something to eat?"

Luke looked again into the almost empty fridge. *Yes, Mom. And for dessert I want you to walk on water.*

"No, Mom, I'll sort myself out."

Luke would probably have said the same thing, even if the fridge was full. His mom, it had to be said, wasn't the greatest chef in New York. It wasn't that she couldn't just boil an egg – or fry, or poach it – she always somehow managed to leave eggshell on it. (Luke used to hate this when he was a kid: the eggshell was the part that touched the hen's ass. His mom reassured him that it actually came out of the hen's vagina.)

"But that's not to say she's not a good mom, Doctor Squires. She's cool. I can talk to her about stuff…Maybe not the stuff you need to talk about to a psychiatrist but stuff about – I don't know – the issues facing the American teenager and whatnot. And she listens too. She really does…I guess she has to. Family is a shitty job you can't resign from."

Luke took an apologetic piece of pie and a stick of celery from the fridge and stuck it on a plate.

"There's some toast on the table, if you want it, Luke," his mom said. "I couldn't eat it. It'll be cold now though."

Luke didn't mind. He found it amusing that people didn't like the idea of eating cold toast, but whenever

they stayed at hotels, they always insisted on finishing
that rack of toast that came with the cooked breakfast –
even though the toast is now freezing cold – purely on
the grounds that they've paid for it.

"Thanks, Mom."

Luke stuck the toast on his plate and headed back
to the safety of his bedroom, before the next
argument kicked in. (There were usually aftershocks.)
He turned on his portable TV. He flicked through the
channels to see if *The Nanny* was on. It wasn't. So he
stuck a Nintendo game into his NES and turned that
on instead.

Nothing happened.

He removed the cartridge, blew on it hastily (like it
was his favorite food he'd just dropped on the carpet)
and reinserted it.

"The Legend of Zelda" appeared.

Luke loved this game. It wasn't like "Super Mario
Bros" – you didn't have to play it in a particular way;
you could move around more freely. It was non-linear.
Luke's brain was non-linear. He skillfully moved around
the dungeons, collecting weapons, stabbing monsters,
eating pie, celery, and cold toast.

"There are lots of tips and cheats on how to play
'The Legend of Zelda,' Doctor Squires, but if you
really want to get good at it, *really* good at it, the
best one is this: don't have any friends. That's how I
did it – but it wasn't intentional. I guess you lose

17

friends the same way you make 'em: it just kinda happens…Although perhaps you could call Justin my friend, but I'm not sure he would. But we *used* to be close."

Luke pressed the pause button and went to find an old yearbook. He rifled through the pages as if he needed to convince himself. It seemed such a long time ago now.

He found the picture he was looking for, and studied it. It was one of him and Justin taken several years ago. They were both wearing sports uniforms, backward, like Kris Kross.

"Oh, yeah, back in the day, me and Jus used to be real tight…"

Luke closed the book.

"I guess everything changes…"

And he went back to "The Legend of Zelda."

"…usually for the worse."

Hours passed. And the Shapiro house eventually became as silent as the street. Luke knew this could only mean one thing: his parents must have fallen asleep. He left his bedroom and crept down the stairs and into the living room. He saw his dad, illuminated by the flickering light of the TV, asleep in his suit on the couch – like he was lying in an open coffin surrounded by candles. Luke turned the TV off…Then he went into his parents' bedroom. His mom was asleep on the bed, also in her clothes, watching the same TV

program. He turned off the light and the TV. And he went back to his room.

"But you're right, Doctor Squires, tomorrow *is* a big day in my life. One of the biggest. Tomorrow my life changes. Tomorrow I graduate. Tomorrow I become a man...And then I go to my fall-back college. And then I get older. And then I die."

three

Luke's mom burst into his bedroom like Kramer; like a rodeo rider without a horse. At least, that's how it seemed to Luke. He immediately stopped what he was doing – meticulously weighing out weed on a digital scale, placing the portions into plastic bags – and stood up in front of his desk, slightly spreading the graduation robe that hung off his shoulders like he was trying to preserve the secrets of the Batcave.

"Look at you!" his mom exclaimed.

"Yes!" Luke said, trying to make his voice go up at the end too. "Look at me!"

Luke wondered why the reward for not graduating was to not look stupid. Fuck knows how he was meant to wear his graduation cap. (Do you wear it like a visor?) He could feel it pushing his brow down, making him look even more pissed off.

"Here," his mom said, "let me sort that out for you."

She took off the cap, swept his thick dark hair away from his face and replaced it, pushing it further back this time.

"Now I can see your beautiful eyes," she said.

(Luke wondered how *she* knew what to do.) She stepped back to look at him. "I am so proud of you... My little graduate."

Her voice didn't go up at the end this time. It trailed off and broke into syllables.

"Mom, don't cry," Luke told her. "You'll only get your nice dress wet."

But tears of joy don't run down the face, they meander – pushed to the sides of the cheeks by a broad grin before barely dripping from the chin. (This was a revelation to Luke.)

"I can't help it," his mom said, taking a tissue from her handbag as she got even more juiced up. "Seeing you like that, my baby, all grown up... I'm just so very proud of you. Do you know that?"

"Yes, Ma, I know it," Luke said, turning her around and shepherding her to the door, wondering how proud she would be if she saw what was on the desk.

She turned her head to look at his face. "Do you? Do you really know?"

"Yes, Ma, I do. Really."

And she was almost at the door when his dad appeared in his sharpest double-breasted suit from the mid-eighties. "Time to go," he announced. "Can't be late for your own graduation, can you, Luke?"

"Just a second," his mom said.

And she retreated into Luke's room to check herself in the long mirror on the wardrobe door. Luke walked backward to the edge of his desk again.

His dad looked at his wife, looked at his watch and sighed – but he couldn't resist joining her in front of the mirror.

Luke watched in amazement as his parents squinted into the mirror, making imperceptible adjustments to buttons and belts; and at their faces as they tried to spot invisible dust on the backs of their shoulders. It looked like they were having a stroke.

At the end of the day, they'd be sleeping in these clothes.

There was only one thing to do with Luke's clothes that bothered him. And throughout the whole graduation ceremony, he was thinking about it.

A couple of years ago, someone had collected his diploma with his flies down. Of course, by the time the story had done the rounds, a testicle was also hanging out. Luke didn't believe that, but he didn't trust these pants either. The zip didn't seem entirely like other zips. It didn't seem as confident as other zips. It didn't make that noise that other zips made – the rising tone on the fastening movement, and the falling note on the

unfastening... Luke wondered whether zips actually made those noises themselves, or whether they just *seemed* to make those noises because the zip was either moving toward or away from you. In any event, the zip on Luke's pants didn't make these noises at all.

Throughout the speeches Luke had checked his flies a dozen times. *They were up. They were definitely up*... But as the headmaster geared himself up to read out the students' names, an irrational thought entered Luke's head and chained itself to his brain: what if the long walk across the stage to collect his diploma somehow managed to work his flies down... And then, what if, somehow, his testicle managed... *No*. The testicle bit wasn't remotely feasible, Luke told himself. That was just paranoia. In all probability. But the flies thing, *that* was possible.

Luke tried to listen to what the headmaster was saying: tried and tested final words designed to give the graduating students the wisdom, guidance, and encouragement they could draw upon throughout the rest of their lives... but nothing that could help Luke get through the next fifteen minutes.

And now the names began.

Luke had seen people walking in the street with their hands behind their backs. Do people ever walk with their hands in front of themselves like that, covering their groin? He considered this question right up until the headmaster announced, "Luke Shapiro!"

Fuck it. Inspired by the enthusiastic applause (from his own family) Luke decided to do an impression of a normal human being for once in his life, and confidently walked, hands by his sides, to collect his diploma – only succumbing once, toward the end, to the temptation to glance down and check that his flies were still up…He stumbled into the headmaster. The laughter was more widespread than the applause. But although it seemed like the worst baton exchange in sprint history, Luke managed to walk away with his diploma in his hand. And despite everything, he still felt a rare feeling of pride as he unrolled the diploma. (The only lingering trace of negativity was the understandable curiosity as to whether they'd given him the right one.)

"'*TUITION FEES OUTSTANDING*,'" Luke read.

(They had.)

"Closer…Closer…A little bit closer, please."

Luke begrudgingly followed the photographer's instruction and shuffled closer to his dad.

"Noticed there was no diploma, Dad," Luke said through a gritted smile.

"I just owe the school a little money, Lucas," his dad smiled back. "Let's not let it ruin a magical day."

A flashbulb popped. And the moment was captured forever.

"Congratulations, Shapiros!" a man's voice called out.

Luke turned round and squinted into the sun. It was Doctor Squires with his wife – Stephanie's mom.

Mrs Squires was tall and slim and dressed in black. She walked ahead of her husband like she was his long-evening shadow. (Her only concession to color was to accessorize her outfit with a cigarette, which she sucked on so hard that – even in the blinding sunshine – it crackled bright red.) Luke had seen her before at various school ceremonies and thought she was seriously beautiful. Or should that be beautifully serious? Despite the fact that she was younger than Doctor Squires, it was as if she could never forget that she wasn't as attractive as she once was, and tomorrow she wouldn't be as attractive as she was now. (Yes, cigarettes were terrible for causing wrinkles, but then again so was smiling. She'd made her choice.)

"Lucas? Aren't you going to introduce us?" Luke's dad asked.

"Right. Mom, Dad. This is Mister Doctor Squires."

Doctor Squires held out his hand. "Jeff – And this is my wife, Kristen."

"A pleasure," Mrs Squires said.

Luke looked up. "And here's your daughter."

As Luke gazed at Stephanie walking across the lawn toward them – watching her beautiful long dark hair and party dress slowly rippling and undulating like she was moving underwater – he wondered why he always saw her in slow motion when, as far as he was concerned, she could never get to him quickly enough. Perhaps, Luke decided, it was because he wanted to stretch the moment out. She was never around him for long.

"Stepdaughter," Doctor Squires corrected Luke.

Stephanie stubbed out her cigarette and held out her hand to Luke's parents.

"Stephanie," she said, with total assurance.

"You must be so proud of your boy, Shapiros," Doctor Squires said.

Luke didn't give his parents time to answer.

"You must be so prouder, Sir," he said. "Your little flower graduated *Come Loudly*, no?"

Stephanie looked down at her shoes to hide her smile, shaking her head.

"How lovely!" Luke's mom said, putting her hands together. "You just missed *Cum Laude*, didn't you, dear?"

Luke shrugged. "I was busy with my after school activities, Ma."

"Yes, Mrs Shapiro," Stephanie said, glancing at Luke mischievously. "Your son has many extra-curricular activities."

"Oh, and what are those, Luke?" his dad said sarcastically. "The yearbook staff seem to have neglected to note your achievements."

Luke shot his dad a look. He'd been forced to dress up in these stupid fucking robes and hat (on what was probably the hottest day of the year so far). He'd had

to listen to six of the worst speeches ever written. He'd tripped on the stage like a cunt. All to receive a bill written in italics on parchment paper... *And now this fucker's scoring off him?!*

"You'll have to ask Steph's pops about that," Luke told him flatly.

"Steppops," Stephanie said.

Luke's dad laughed nervously, unsure what they meant. And what to say next.

"Alright, team – picture time," Doctor Squires announced as the photographer set up a Shapiro–Squires family portrait.

"Closer... Closer..."

Everyone shuffled.

"A little bit closer."

More movement ensued.

"A little bit..."

"Why don't you just step back a bit instead?" Mrs Squires told the photographer.

He looked up from his camera, wounded. And duly obliged.

"And tuck your fuckin' shirt in, Jeffrey," she told her husband.

Doctor Squires glanced across at Luke... then looked down to tuck in his shirt. Just as a flashbulb popped.

four

"This guy's going to ruin the city," Doctor Squires said, watching the TV.

Mayor Giuliani was holding a press conference. Doctor Squires was holding a cocktail.

"I said, 'This guy's going to…'"

"Yes, Jeffrey, I heard what you said," Mrs Squires told her husband, as she walked through to their bedroom in her underwear, carrying the black dress she'd worn from that day's graduation ceremony. "I'm sure the Mayor is just trying to clean up the city."

"Yeah, well – I like it dirty… I like it messy."

Mrs Squires disappeared into the bedroom.

"Hey, Kristen," Doctor Squires called out to her. "Have you seen my stash? I can't find it."

"No, I haven't," Mrs Squires called back. "And you shouldn't smoke grass in the house anyway."

"The kids call it pot."

"Well, you're not a kid. So stop smoking it or I'll call Mayor Giuliani and he'll drag you downtown."

Doctor Squires looked round their opulent penthouse.

"Couldn't be much worse than this place," he said to himself.

But as he spotted his bag of weed on the floor – half-hidden behind the base of a lampstand – his mood lightened. For a second. It was empty.

He picked up the phone again.

"Where *is* that kid?"

Mrs Squires was sitting alone in their bedroom obsessing about their single friends, when her husband walked in.

"A beautiful night!" he announced, like he was toasting it with his cocktail.

"Uh-huh."

"Whatcha doing?"

She nodded at the computer screen. "The seating for that charity thing," she told him.

"What charity thing?" Doctor Squires asked.

"You know, the children's charity thing."

"Oh. The children's charity thing," Doctor Squires said, stressing the new word as if it now all made sense to him.

His wife carried on typing.

Doctor Squires sat on the bed. "You know, the other day, this kid in the street – he couldn't have been more than eight years old – he called me a 'motherfucker.' Can you believe that?"

"What did you say?"

"I told him he'd been in his mother's cunt a damn sight more recently than I'd been in mine."

"That's very good, Jeffrey."

Doctor Squires got off the bed and strolled over to the bedroom window. "Such a beautiful night."

"So you keep saying."

"You wanna go out?"

She stopped typing.

"Out?" she asked him.

Doctor Squires nodded.

"I told you, Jeffrey, I'm doing the seating for the..."

"Yes, for the children's charity thing. But do you want to go out?"

"I take it you didn't find your grass or pot or whatever the fuck you want to call it."

"No – although I think I know what happened to it – but that's not why I want us to go out... Can't you just seat them anywhere?"

"The married couples, yes, they *have* to sit together. But the single people..."

"Come on, Kristen. Let's just go out. Grab a drink. Chill."

She began typing again.

"It's a Tuesday night," she said. "And I'm forty."

"Two," Doctor Squires said, leaving the bedroom. "You're forty-two."

Stephanie was putting on make-up, listening to "Flower" by Liz Phair, when there was a knock on her bedroom door.

"Yeah?"

The door opened.

"Hey," Doctor Squires said.

"Hey," she said back.

"Stephanie, um – you don't happen to have any extra pot lying around, do you?"

Stephanie laughed.

"What's so funny?"

"Nothing. It's just – you called the weed pot."

"Oh…Well, do you have any extra weed? The dog ate mine again."

At Doctor Squires's feet, there was a very stoned-looking west highland terrier; he cocked his head quizzically.

"No," Stephanie told him. "You try Shapiro?"

"I've been paging him…He's probably with his friends. Celebrating."

"He'll call back."

"He hasn't so far."

"Well, you could always wait for the dog to fart."

"Very funny."

"Don't worry. He'll call back."

"Where are you going, anyway?"

"Out."

"Uh-huh…Well, don't be back too late."

Stephanie looked at him as quizzically as the dog. "Right."

Doctor Squires closed the bedroom door behind him and headed for the bathroom. (The west highland terrier had tried to follow him and given up halfway down the hall.) He locked the bathroom door and sat on the edge of their huge bath, which incorporated high power massage body jets, a headrest, and gold plated taps – and which his wife had installed to replace the walk in shower.

Doctor Squires preferred showers to baths. He could never really tell whether the water was too hot or too cold, and at least in a shower, the first thing to feel it was the top of his head. As he lowered himself into a bath, however, it was the most sensitive parts of his body that felt it first: his feet, his balls, his asshole...

Doctor Squires was feeling sensitive.

He stood up and went to the bathroom cabinet. It was full of bottles of prescription pharmaceuticals. His hands moved over them, like he was a factory worker tightening lids on an assembly line. Finally, he found the bottle he was looking for. He unscrewed the top, popped a pill and put the bottle back into the cabinet, making sure that the label – printed with the word "Lithium" – was facing forward this time.

Where *was* that kid?

five

Luke licked his hand and patted down the errant hair like a cat grooming itself. He could see his reflection in the polished brass number on the front of the door to the swanky SoHo apartment – and he could hear the party was in full swing on the other side of it.

He rang the doorbell.

Even before the chime had finished, the door had swung open.

Justin appeared, a cigarette dangling from the corner of his mouth.

"You paged me?" Luke asked him.

Justin looked from side to side before taking Luke by the arm. "Get in here."

Before Luke knew it, he'd been marched into a bathroom. Justin locked the door behind them, and rattled the handle just to make sure.

"I didn't know there was a party here tonight," Luke said.

"It's a graduation party," Justin told him.

"I just graduated."

"Yeah. I know."

"So, can I grab a beer or something?"

"Naw, man. They can't see you here."

"Why not?"

"Cuz you weren't invited."

"But I'm your friend. You invited me."

Justin shook his head. "I don't have inviting privileges, man."

"But…"

"Shapiro. I paged you…remember?"

Luke opened his backpack and pulled out a couple of different sized bags of weed.

Justin opened his wallet. "Hey, can you spot me thirty dollars?"

Luke shook his head. "Just take it."

Justin tried to hand him the few dollar bills from his wallet.

"No," Luke told him. "I don't want your four dollars. Obviously. Just take it."

"Good lookin' out," Justin said, granting Luke half a smile (the cigarette was pulling the other corner of his mouth down). "This should last us till the first Amsterdam weekend."

"You're going to Amsterdam?"

"Yeah, man. I told you, Rollo and I are going to Europe to sample the culture – and to try to bang American art history students."

"You never told me that."

"Yes I did."

"And you're gonna take it on the plane?"

"I'll put it in my shoe. They never check that shit."

Luke's pager vibrated. He checked it. "Can I at least use the phone?" he asked.

Justin's shoulders slumped. "Come on, man. You don't wanna be here anyway. This party's wack. Trust me. I'm about to be out myself. I just need to find a girl to bone. So, unless you can help me with that…"

Luke zipped up his backpack again.

"I really appreciate it," Justin said.

"No problem…Well, have a nice summer, I guess."

Luke went to open the bathroom door.

"Wait…" Justin said.

Luke whipped his head round expectantly.

"I'll just check if it's clear for you to leave, Shapiro."

He disappeared out of the bathroom, leaving Luke standing there. He looked at himself in the huge bathroom mirror. That lock of hair on the top of his head was still sticking up. It looked like the fuse on a cartoon bomb. It didn't seem to matter now…And yet, deep down, he didn't blame Justin for wanting to keep his distance: when people are always laughing at someone – and you're standing next to them – kinda feels like some of it is landing on you.

The bathroom door opened again. But it wasn't Justin.

"Oh. Shapiro. Sorry."

"No, Stephanie, it's cool. Hey."

Luke casually ran his fingers through his hair, trying to make it all stick up.

"What are you doing here, Shapiro?"

"Here at the party, or here in the bathroom?"

"Both, I guess."

"Well, I'm not really at the party – Justin paged me. And what I'm doing in the bathroom is…waiting, I guess…Hiding, maybe?"

"Who are you hiding from?"

"Oh, no one in particular. I don't think…Justin's checkin' if the coast is clear. You know, the way bodyguards do for celebrities?"

Luke smiled to himself at the thought of how the extremities of popularity could sometimes meet in the middle. Or in a bathroom.

Stephanie pulled out a pill from one of the front pockets of her jeans, and an ATM card from the other. She started to cut up a line on the counter, between the two sinks.

She turned round to Luke. "Ritalin?"

Luke shook his head.

"You sure?"

"Really. I'm cool…Besides, I don't wanna be made any smarter. I hear that smart kids can be very unpopular in high schools."

"You just graduated."

"I thought so, yeah."

Luke watched as Stephanie bent over to snort the white powder. The top of her jeans and the bottom of her shirt pulled apart from each other, revealing soft golden down on her tanned lower back.

When she resurfaced, her eyes were watering.

"You got a cigarette?" she asked.

Luke handed her a pack. She took a cigarette and handed the pack back.

"I quit," he said, balancing the temptation to have something she'd held, with the desire to give her something of his.

"You quit?" she asked.

"Think so. I just quit."

Stephanie shrugged and put the pack into her front pocket along with her ATM card.

"You feel different?" Luke asked her.

"From the Ritalin, or the graduation?"

"The graduation."

"Nope...Do you feel different, Shapiro?"

"No more than usual."

"Fuck it," Stephanie said, checking herself in the mirror. "We have our whole lives to feel different."

She pulled her shirt tight and pushed her tits out. Luke watched small creases radiate from around the straining buttons like starbursts.

"Whatcha doin' after tonight?" she asked him.

"I'm thinking of taking a gap year."

"Really? What are you going to do?"

"Work at Gap."

Stephanie smiled and shook her head, the way she had at the graduation. "Actually, I meant what are you doing for the summer?"

"Chillin'. Making money… Why? You wanna go steady?"

"Yeah. Sure," she deadpanned back.

There was silence for a while. But Luke had become curious.

"What are you doing?" he asked her. "For the summer?"

"I'm interning for one of Stepdaddy's patients."

"Who is he?"

"That's confidential," she said. "But he runs Miramax."

"That's awesome. Congratulations."

Luke had thought about interning – but all the posts had wanted office skills. (He didn't think he could pass "sticking a porno mag under a mattress" as "experience of filing.")

"So I guess we'll both be here all summer, huh?" Luke said. "All alone."

"Yeah, but we'll never hang out."

"Oh."

There was another silence. This time it was broken by Stephanie.

"You know, now that you're at the party, you may as well stay."

"*Don't go putting thoughts in his head.*" Justin appeared at the doorway.

"Oh, come on, Justin," Stephanie said. "It's fine."

Justin looked at them like they were both insane.

six

"CONGRATULATIONS CLASS OF 1994."

The huge banner ran across almost the entire length of the roof garden. Below it, everyone was drinking, laughing, and dancing close. And above it, Luke was perched on the water tower alone.

The warm feeling that had come over him when Justin said he could stay had been like peeing in the sea. He'd soon felt cold again.

Why did he think it would be different to before?

If anything, it was *worse* now – being so close to everything...

Luke looked down at all his classmates moving to "Bring da Ruckus" by Wu-Tang Clan, and he wished he could lose himself in the center of that warm sticky mass of people. He yearned to feel a connection between himself, the music, and other human beings.

This was why he preferred his boombox to his walkman: he wanted to share that which was so important to him. *More* important to him. He looked at

all his classmates dancing with such passion to the music, such commitment… but you never saw anyone in a club past the age of thirty dancing like that. Why not? If music had meant so much to them when they were younger, why did they abandon it? It was always the way – the young are full of shit. But Luke knew he was different. He was loyal. He still listened to cassettes.

And yet, he knew that even if he had the courage to walk down there – and even if that mass of people didn't repel him – it would only make it worse for himself. Like animals engaging in a pre-mating ritual, dancing should be sign-language for "Fuck me," not "Help me" – and Luke danced like Bambi trying to stand up. He'd seen better dancing in church. And this was another consequence of having no friends: he'd missed out on learning all the important social skills that don't so much get you through life, as enable you to *have* a life; skills which everybody else had learned years ago. (Luke was convinced that had his balls known who they were attached to, they wouldn't have bothered dropping. Puberty had been an amazing act of optimism on his body's behalf.)

Luke sparked up a joint and took a big hit.

He looked away from the decking area which was serving as a dance floor and picked out individual people below him. There was Christine and Simone. They were tall and thin and always stood close together

– they reminded Luke of the writing at the bottom of film posters – and they were forever whispering into each other's ears. Luke imagined what they were saying, actually seeing their words in the form of movie subtitles:

"You know, Shapiro has to deal dope because his family's stony broke."

"*Stoner Broke.* That would be a good nickname for him."

"Nah, let's stick to *Fuckin' Loser.*"

He looked across at a smirking Rollo, and imagined his subtitles as he talked to a girl:

"Shapiro's never gonna get laid."

"I know. I can't believe he actually stayed… Look at him up there, hanging around like a bad fart."

"Oh, I know. Look at his hair sticking up from the top of his head like an erect penis. He looks ridiculous."

"He looks *ri-cock-ulous.*"

"Well, I hope there isn't a storm. It's gonna act like a lightning conductor. On second thoughts, I hope there is a storm."

"Me too."

Right on cue, they both burst into thunderous laughter. Even carrying on laughing when there was no noise left; bent over double, the need to laugh overriding the need to breathe.

Then Stephanie walked over to them:

"Actually, I think Shapiro's…"

Luke strained to see what the rest of her subtitle said. The words were forming slowly. He leant forward, but Rollo walked across obscuring her words with his own:

"YO – LET'S FUCK!"

Luke shook his head and stubbed out his joint. He pushed himself up to his feet and descended from his perch. It felt like he was climbing down from a rooftop protest in a prison – and he thought back to what Doctor Squires had said in his office yesterday: that he'd mark today with no more joy than a prisoner counting his sentence making a diagonal line on the wall of his cell.

Luke kept his eyes on his sneakers as he made his way to the hallway and rang for the elevator.

The door opened.

And there was Justin with a joint in his mouth, sucking back the weed that Luke had given him, and some teenage girl that Luke had never seen before, sucking on his cock. She'd immediately stopped what she was doing when the doors had opened – and began licking his balls and tossing his shaft.

"I'll take the stairs," Luke said, turning away.

But right before the doors closed, Justin called out to him.

"Have a good summer, Shapiro!"

seven

Luke awoke the next morning with a raging thirst/headache/hard on.

He didn't know which to deal with first...

Distraction therapy dealt with all three.

He quickly dressed and went downstairs. (It must have been serious; they were arguing in the front room.)

"How am I supposed to live?" his mom was screaming at his dad. "How am I supposed to function?"

"You're not," his dad told her.

The casualness of her husband's reply momentarily shocked her – and the horrible noise which normally flowed between them like bagpipes was broken with an uncharacteristic pause as her mouth opened and closed as silently as a goldfish.

Luke's entrance into the front room saved her from articulation. She dashed toward her son as soon as she saw him.

"Your father lost all our money," she said. "We have to move to – I don't know, somewhere poor."

"*We're moving?*"

"Lucas, I'm your father, and I promise you – we are not getting evicted."

"*We're getting evicted?*"

"No! I'll fix it," his dad told him, before looking sternly at his wife. "We've got plenty of time."

Luke's mom scoffed. "Yeah. Plenty. Two months, Luke. Two months! This is the whole problem with your father, Luke. He thinks it takes the same amount of time to fix things as it does for him to screw them up."

"Your mother and I are getting a divorce, Luke."

"Don't you dare tell him that! That's not even true…That's not true, honey."

It never ceased to amaze Luke how for those few seconds that they turned to him, like he was Judge Wapner on *The People's Court*, they could immediately lose the anger and the hatred and talk rationally – but they were incapable of exercising any self-control for each other.

His dad approached him. "Yes, it is true, Luke. We are getting a divorce. Your mother is a raving lunatic. She's only with me for my money. And I don't have any money now."

Wide-eyed and wordless, Luke's mom was again transformed into a goldfish.

His dad put his hand on Luke's shoulder. "I want you to remember this, son: failure is male rape. No matter how unjust it is, women will always suspect it was somehow your fault."

His mom blinked. "It *was* your fault! You lost all our money!"

Luke suddenly noticed the scratches on his dad's face. Some had broken the skin, others had merely dragged it. They ran down his cheeks like red and white tears.

"What happened to your face, Dad?"

He turned to his mom.

"What happened to his face?"

His mom looked down, biting her nails as if she were trying to eat the evidence.

"Did you fucking scratch him?" Luke asked her.

His mom was silent.

Luke shook his head in disbelief, yet at the same time he acknowledged there was a horrible logic to this escalation: they couldn't afford to smash crockery any more. But still, he had to hear her say it.

"*Mom, did you scratch him?*"

"He hit me," she said.

"I did not, you goddamned liar!…Don't ever hit a woman, Luke."

Luke looked at them both. "You guys are acting like you're fucking twelve years old."

"Stop cursing," his mom told him.

"Fuck off!"

Luke stormed off back to his bedroom, slammed his door, and gave them the finger with both hands so vigorously, and so many times, it looked like he was juggling with invisible balls. Exhausted, he threw himself down onto his still warm bed and wished that he'd never woken up. Ever.

But, seeing as he had, he knew he had to be practical.

He rolled off the bed and retrieved a shoebox from under it. He removed the lid. There was a stack of twenty-dollar bills. "Your income is X. Your outgoings are Y," Luke said to himself, taking out some money. "$X - Y =$ How happy you are." Or, at least, that's how it seemed to be with his parents.

When Luke went downstairs, his mom was sitting alone in the living room, watching *The Jerry Springer Show* on TV. The guests were beeping like R2-D2, and his mom was staring intently at the screen as if she desperately needed to see people whose situation was worse than their own. (She hadn't seen any yet.)

Luke approached her holding a couple of twenties. "For dinner," he said.

His mom smiled and blinked slowly, touched by his gesture.

"Oh, honey," she said. "I can't take that from you."

Luke dropped the money and turned on his heel before it had fluttered to the floor.

"Where are you going?" his mom asked.

"To try to sort things out…"

eight

"I've been paging you for days, Luke."

"This isn't a monogamous relationship, Doctor Squires, I do have other clients."

Luke took out a couple of bags of weed from his backpack and slid them across the mahogany desk.

"It's not a pizza," Luke told him. "You gotta be patient."

Doctor Squires picked up the bags and nodded.

"Listen, Doctor Squires," Luke said, shuffling forward in his chair. "I got a question for you. And it's kind of important."

"Tell me, Luke."

"So can you, like, prescribe medicine and shit?"

"Of course."

"Cuz some people – psychiatrists..."

"Psychologists."

"I've been researching it. They can't."

"Well, I can," Doctor Squires said, flicking one hand over his shoulder at the certificates on the wall, while pointing the other to the prescription pad on the table, like he was performing semaphore. "Why do you ask?"

"It's for me."

"No shit."

"Well, I think, recently, that I'm depressed."

"Recently, Luke?"

"For the last three years or so...I don't sleep so good. And when I do sleep – well, even after a nightmare, it's painful to wake up...And I *think*, Doctor Squires! I think way too much. I obsess about things. Sometimes the smallest thing..."

"What do you think about?"

"*Shit!* That's what I think about."

"Give me an example, Luke."

"Okay, the other night my mom's sittin' in the kitchen in the dark with a headache. And I can see by the light of the fridge that she's got her eyes closed, and she's squeezin' her temples with her fingers. And I'm concerned about her. Fuck! Of course I'm concerned about her. But what I also can't help thinking about is the light that's coming out from the fridge. You gotta change bulbs all over the apartment, but you never got to change that bulb in the fridge. I don't know what bulbs they put in fridges, but I'm thinkin' they wanna make those bulbs for the rest of the apartment...You see, Doctor Squires? *Shit!*"

"You ever heard the saying, 'The unexamined life is not worth living?'"

"Woody Allen?"

"Socrates...He was a philosopher."

Luke sighed. He came here to try to make Doctor Squires see how he really felt. He came here to show him that his life wasn't just screwed, it was gang-raped. He came here for drugs, and Doctor Squires was giving him philosophy. What fuckin' use was philosophy? The only way Luke was gonna acquire any depth was by jumping into the East River from the top of the Manhattan Bridge.

"Fine, Doctor Squires, you say the unexamined life is not worth living?"

"Not me, Luke. Socra..."

"Whoever. Well, maybe the examined life isn't worth living either."

"Don't talk like that...Luke, tell me, does this have anything to do with Kurt Cobain?"

Luke sighed again.

"The point is, Doctor Squires, who says it all has to be so sad like this, you know?"

"Is something going on, Luke...at home?"

Luke slumped back into his chair. "Of course something's going on at home. This is what you get paid for?"

"Perhaps you'd be better off seeing a psychic, son."

Luke looked downwards. "I don't really want to talk about it."

"Men do the things they need to do, to become the men they want to be. Do you understand?"

"Uh-huh."

Doctor Squires lowered his head, tilting it, so as to attract Luke's gaze. "That includes asking for help," he said.

"It's my parents," Luke told him.

"There you go. What about them?"

Luke thought for a while.

"You know what, Doctor Squires, forget it. It's boring."

"What's boring?"

"Bitching about your parents. Kids blame their parents for everything – from the underachievement to the overbite – it's totally played out. It's like *listening* to paint dry."

"Very well."

"It's just… they act like kids, you know?"

"My wife and I are the same way. We act like kids all the time."

"Why do you think that is?"

"I don't know. Maybe we never change – and when we grow up there's no one to stop us acting like kids any more… Or maybe it's just life. It has a funny way of turning us into the one thing we don't want to be."

Luke nodded. "Very wise…" Then he leant forward again. "Doctor Squires, I want to tell you about my life. My life sucks. When I'm not at school or dealing drugs, I spend all my time playing 'The Legend of Zelda.'"

"What's 'The Legend of Zelda?'"

"It's a video game. You collect weapons, you kill monsters, there's some role playing. It's basically 'Dungeons and Dragons' for people with no friends."

"What's 'Dungeons and Dragons?'"

"That's not important, Doctor Squires. Didn't you hear what I said? I have no friends in New York – or anywhere for that matter. Do you know what that's like? To be seventeen and have no friends?"

Doctor Squires didn't know what that was like. When he was at school he had friends. But, like many people, he'd gone from school friends, to work friends, to spending time with his family. Each year, his world had become smaller – as did the conversation – until finally the walls started closing in. In the bad weather, he didn't mind it so much. He could almost convince himself it felt kind of cozy. But it was during the summer that he felt it the most. On a hot summer's day – a day like today – he wanted nothing more than to sit outside a bar with a cold beer and someone to talk to… And so sometimes, on such days, desperation would lead him to put aside all sense of embarrassment, and he'd pick up the phone and call someone that he used to know… Of course, they wouldn't be interested. Friendship is like a garden: once neglected it becomes overgrown, unmanageable. No one wants to tackle an awkward job like that. Not on a summer's day.

"I understand it more than you think, son," Doctor Squires told him.

"But at least you have a wife. I have no girlfriend. I have no girl who will even look at me, other than my mom…Doctor Squires, *I slouch on the subway trying to see up women's skirts.*"

Doctor Squires looked at him. "And…?"

"And that's not good! I'm disgusted with my behavior. My whole life repulses me. Basically, I'm just trying to get to college before I put a bullet in my brain."

Doctor Squires shook his head at what he was hearing.

"Lucas, do you know what I would give to be you again? Not you, specifically, but me at your age? It doesn't get any better."

"Please tell me that's not true."

"But it *is* true. And it doesn't make any sense either, because the older you get, the more you act sensibly and cautiously – as if you've got more to lose, when, in fact, every day you have *less*. The young, on the other hand, they live each day as if it were their last. *That's* what you should be doing."

"I do, Doctor Squires, but only because I live in hope."

"You're fucking living, Luke. It's a great thing, living. Go out there and get your heart broken. Find yourself face down in the gutter. Get your pulse up. Make a true mess of yourself, son."

"That what you tell all your patients?"

"You're not depressed, Luke. You're sad. There's a difference."

Luke looked down at his sneakers and thought for a while.

"No, Doctor Squires," he finally said, "I'm depressed. Very depressed. So can't you just give me some happy pills and we'll call it a day?"

"I'm sorry, Luke. I can't do that."

"It's because I'm not lying on the couch, isn't it?"

"Luke…"

"Can't you see what my life is like? At the end of the day, my head is sore from all the thinking. And my lips are cracked from constantly talking to myself. My misery is endless, Doctor Squires, just when I think it might be over, it grows a knuckle and starts again."

"It's very sad that you feel that way, Luke."

"No, Doctor Squires, it's very depressing."

"Luke, I can't prescribe you pills when you're not…"

"Sad. Depressed. What difference does it make if it feels the same?"

"It makes every difference."

"Then how do you suggest I deal?"

"I suggest you talk about it. With a friend."

"Like I said, I don't have any friends."

"You have me."

Luke looked at Doctor Squires. "That's…great."

Luke stood up, threw his backpack onto his shoulders, and went to leave. But he stopped at the door. "What about you?" he asked.

"What about me?"

"Are you depressed or sad?"

Doctor Squires held a lighter to his bong. "I'm both."

nine

When Luke walked out of Doctor Squires's subdued office and into the street, his pupils shrank to the size of amebas, even though he was wearing his visor. He stood in the shade of the doorway to acclimatize to the light – and to the noise, which today seemed especially bad.

As his vision recovered, he discovered why.

A cyclist on the other side of the road was wobbling along in the busy traffic being pursued by a volley of car horns from the car behind that wanted to pass him. Luke could see that at the point where the cycle's wheels met the road, the tires were spreading outwards, like the setting sun seemed to do when it met the horizon. It was almost as if the tarmac and the tires were melting together in the burning heat; then struggling to pull away from each other like cheese on a pizza... Or, maybe the tires simply didn't have enough air in them. (Being depressed is like cycling on deflated tires, Luke thought. It makes you slow and you feel everything.)

In either case, when the cyclist stopped at the lights, the car pulled up alongside him and the driver began to berate him. The cyclist shrugged. And the driver cursed him even more. The cyclist cupped his ear to show that he couldn't hear what he was saying, and the driver reluctantly wound down the window of his air conditioned car … And the cyclist punched him in the face so hard the driver's ears wobbled.

Just another summer's day in New York.

Luke stepped out from the doorway.

"Shapiro!"

Luke turned round. It was Stephanie walking down the street with a west highland terrier on a lead.

"Steph. Hi," Luke said. "Who's the little guy?"

"This is Jesus Christ. From my stepdad's first marriage."

Luke knelt down to fuss him. He liked west highland terriers – with their cute little faces and white wiry hair – they reminded him of his grandparents.

Stephanie looked over at the commotion across the street. "What's all that about?"

"The connection between temper and temperature, I think," Luke told her, not looking away from the dog. "It's gotta be ninety degrees in the shade today, right?"

"I guess … So, what are you doing here?"

"Uh, your stepdad paged me."

"That guy smokes more weed than I do."

"You like him?"

"Doctor Squires? Not really. He gives me a ton of money, though. But you should hear about some of the fucked up people who come into that guy's office."

Luke shot up. "He tells you that shit?"

"Sure."

"He's not supposed to tell you that. There's confidentiality."

"Well, he does. Like this one guy he sees is a chronic masturbator."

"No way! That's crazy. He didn't – um – tell you this guy's name, did he?"

"The guy masturbates seven times a day. And even when he's drained his nuts, he just lies in bed with his hands in his pants. He got fired from work because of it. And one time, he started jerking off in Doctor Squires's office."

Luke exhaled. "What a freak."

"I don't think my mom likes him very much either...Doctor Squires, I mean. Not the masturbating guy. *Jesus Christ! No!*"

Jesus Christ had lifted his leg and begun to urinate on the wheel of an ice cream cart that was chained to a lamppost. Stephanie put her cigarette in her mouth and pulled on the lead with both hands, but to no avail.

"That's okay," Luke said, taking a key from his pocket and unlocking the padlock.

Stephanie looked at the cart. "This thing's yours?"

59

"Uh-huh."

"This is how you said you were gonna be making money this summer?"

"That's right."

"Well, you know what they say, Shapiro. Power is the greatest aphrodisiac."

Luke smiled. "This is just a cover. Take a look."

He checked no one was around, flipped up the top of the cart and opened one of the huge tubs of ice cream that was in it. It was filled with weed.

"It's ninety degrees in the shade," Luke said. "People gotta chill."

"Cool," Stephanie said, her eyes widening as she looked at the concealed drugs. "It's like a Trojan Horse."

"More of a mule, really," he said.

Luke closed it all up again. He knew the air was filling with the smell of weed, but all he could smell was Stephanie's hair. He'd never stood this close to her before.

"Well, that explains why Jesus Christ was so keen to mark his territory," Stephanie told him.

Luke looked puzzled.

"Never mind," Stephanie said. "Where d'you get this cart from anyway?"

Luke had actually found it in the basement of their apartment when they moved in. He was just a little kid then, and his dad had wanted to throw it out, but Luke had asked him if he could keep it. He said that when

he was older, he'd use it for a summer job – to help his parents with the cost of sending him to college. He'd kept his promise.

"I won it in a poker game from an Italian ice cream vendor," Luke said. "I think he had Mafia connections."

Stephanie looked at him suspiciously. "Really?"

"Okay, Steph, you got me … I won it from his monkey. It's hard to bluff when your tail keeps swishing."

Stephanie shook her head. "You are so lame, Shapiro."

"I know," Luke said.

"So … how does it work with this thing?" she asked, running her hand over the top of the cart.

"You could come out with me now, if you like."

"Cool. I'll just take Jesus Christ up to my stepdad."

Luke knelt down again to fuss him good-bye. The dog smelt vaguely of urine. He reminded Luke even more of his grandparents now.

ten

"Hey, I'm not going to get arrested, am I?" Stephanie asked.

"Everything will be fine," Luke told her. "Just act calm and follow my lead."

He pushed his cart away from the direction of the more wide open spaces of Central Park (that were filled with children's laughter and parental threats), and into a secluded area that was made even more so during the summer months when all the trees got snotted up. In fact, you could almost forget you were in the city at all. Only the tops of New York's tallest, squarest, skyscrapers could still impose themselves on this natural landscape: they stuck out from above the treetops like headstones on overgrown graves.

Stephanie looked over her shoulder again. "You're absolutely sure I'm not gonna get in trouble for this?"

"Absolutely," Luke said. "If the cops turn up, we both blame each other and they can't prove anything, right?"

Stephanie looked at him.

"I'm jokin', Steph, you'll be fine…Here, just relax."

Luke pressed play on the boombox that was attached to his cart – and "Summertime" by DJ Jazzy Jeff & the Fresh Prince rose into the trees like urban blossom as they walked on. Stephanie smiled.

"You're not concerned at all about doing this, are you, Shapiro?"

"Oh, on the contrary, I'm worried all the time."

"What about?"

"That someone's gonna ask me for an ice cream."

A voice called out from behind them.

"Luke…! Luke…!"

Luke turned round. "That's her."

A girl emerged from the trees like a woodland nymph. She was tiny and the hem of her white hippie dress dragged along the ground, leaving a trail of long summer grass to spring up behind her as if it had just bowed to its faerie queen as she passed…And as she got closer, Luke could hear the brightly colored beads on the end of her white-girl dreadlocks clack together, as she excitedly ran toward him like a child seeing a parent at the school gates. It was hard to believe they were the same age.

"Hi, Union," Luke said.

"Hi, Luke! This is Albert. We…"

Union ran back to collect Albert, who was strolling along behind her, playing the bongos. She took Albert by the arm and pulled him forward as if she were showing off a picture she'd done that day.

"We just ate mushrooms at the zoo," Union continued. "Albert's very mature."

"Mature?" Albert said, shaking his head. "No. I just know enough to know that there is so much that I do not know."

Union's eyes lit up. "See? He's awesome. Go on, Albert, tell them why you only wear tank tops."

"Nah, they don't wanna hear that – okay, I'll tell them: *an armpit is easier to wash than a T-shirt.*"

"He saves a fortune on laundry costs," Union said. "He's at college."

"I just finished my second Freshman year," Albert said.

"I'm just heading into my first, myself," Luke told him.

Albert squirmed. "College is a buzzkill, man. You should stay in the city. You got a good thing going here..."

"Right..." Luke said. "So...how much do y'all want again?"

"We met at a Phish concert," Union said. "And we saw each other and it was like that episode of *90210* when Brandon and Emily Valentine take ecstasy."

"Euphoria," Stephanie said.

Union looked confused.

"It's called euphoria," Stephanie told her.

Albert started pounding on the bongos. "Euphoria. Runs. Fast. Past. This. Swollen. Place."

"Did you do something to your hair, Luke?" Union asked.

"Uh, no."

"You look cuter. You look like Jason Priestley like that…Albert, doesn't he look like Jason Priestley?"

Albert stopped playing his bongos. "Who?"

Stephanie looked annoyed. "Yo, listen, Onion, there's mad cops out here so let's do this quick, okay?"

A woman's voice came from behind the door.

"Who's the broad? Is she a pig?"

"No," Luke said. "This is Stephanie. She's cool… Stephanie, this is Eleanor."

"Nice to meet you," Stephanie said to the peephole.

The door replied with the sound of a train going over the tracks as multiple locks were turned one after the other, before finally opening.

"She's hot," Eleanor said, as she stood in her doorway.

Luke nodded, embarrassed.

"Sorry about the pig thing," Eleanor said. "I've just been hearing all these nightmare stories about Giuliani. And I had to do it today, cuz I have a guy coming into town tomorrow and we have nothing to talk about unless we're stoned but he fucks like…well…he's a nice guy. Actually, he's a fucking asshole, but here we are."

Stephanie smiled, and they followed Eleanor into her incense filled apartment. Luke noticed that the Paisley pattern on Eleanor's long dress was almost identical to the markings on the sides of the slinking tabby that walked in between her bare feet. In many ways, Eleanor reminded Luke of Union, or specifically of how he imagined Union would be twenty-five years from now, when her love of Central Park and the zoo would be replaced with a window box and a cat. (You can be young and kooky; past a certain age, they call it eccentric.)

Eleanor cleared away the piles of books and news-papers so Luke and Stephanie could sit on the couch, while she sat with her legs crossed in a hanging wicker chair. The cat jumped into her lap, but wasn't content to nestle into this human cradle, and instead insisted on climbing up Eleanor's body – using her navel as a foot hole – to lick her nose and rub its face against hers.

"He's just woken up," Eleanor explained. "And cats aren't like us. They're not hung up about the difference between dreams and reality. To them, they really have been away... Of course, this asshole I've got coming to stay, he's not even too keen on me having a cat in the apartment. He doesn't like me emptying the cat litter tray down the toilet."

"Why not?" Luke asked. "Doesn't it all just flush away?"

"Some of the gravel doesn't. He says it's like shitting in a goldfish bowl. Personally, I think he's just

intimidated by our relationship. But it's like I tell him: the outpouring of love you have for a pet – the love which overflows – *that's* the love you give to other animals. This is why you can never love them enough... Or maybe it's just *me* he finds intimidating. Am I intimidating, Luke? Am I intimidating to men because I play an instrument?"

"No," Luke said. "...You play an instrument?"

"Yes, Luke. I'm a musician. God, you don't know anything about me."

"I mean, I don't really need to...know anything about you."

"I was in a band, Luke: 'Emergency Breakthrough.' We were big in the eighties. Well, we were big in 1982. Jesus, you know nothing about music."

"Sure I do."

"Hip hop is not music, Luke. It is noise...Please tell me I don't look as old as I sound. Fuck it. I don't care. You see these wrinkles around my eyes? I got them from smiling at cats."

Eleanor stood up and went into the kitchen. The cat followed her...Luke couldn't see what she'd brought back with her, but the cat insisted on walking directly under it – the plastic bowl hovering over his head like a halo – as if to make sure it didn't get away. She put the bowl down. It looked like cat milk, and the cat lapped it up quickly – droplets ending up on the ends of his whiskers. They looked like deeley boppers.

He set about cleaning himself, starting with the troublesome tail…

"Men have a similar relationship to their penises as cats have to their tails," Eleanor said. "They're not really in control of them."

She turned to Stephanie.

"What about you, darling?" she asked. "What's your insight into guys? Do you think it's possible to find a man who's attracted to a woman's mind, or do they all just wanna fuck her brains out…? Why am I asking? Of course you don't know. You picked a real handful with this one."

Luke and Stephanie looked at each other.

"Oh. We're…"

"Not."

"That."

They replied consecutively.

"Really?" Eleanor asked.

"Really," Luke told her. "We're just… We just know each other from high school."

"Well, that's a shame," Eleanor said. "You guys have real good chemistry. You should try doing it one time – just to see how it feels."

Luke looked at her. "You know, Eleanor, it's lovely to talk to you an' all, but you can really just tell me how much you want and leave it at that."

"Fifty of the bubble gum, please."

Stephanie didn't say much, as Luke walked her back to her home. Luke didn't blame her. He blamed himself. How could he have been so dumb as to suggest that Stephanie come out with him as he dealt? He could've just explained how it worked. Fuck. It would've taken him all of five seconds. He had an ice cream cart filled with drugs and a boombox. He sold to hippies around the Meadow, kids uptown, older folks by the zoo. End of story. But oh no! He had to invite Stephanie out with him to give her probably the most pointless and uncomfortable afternoon of her life, *because that would make her like him more, wouldn't it?* Why didn't he just go home and dye his hair ginger?

Hell is custom made, Luke decided. There isn't anything that we didn't choose for ourselves.

What made matters worse was that, deep down, he knew why he'd done it (and it wasn't just to spend the afternoon with Stephanie): he wanted her to see him with other people; people who called him Luke and not Shapiro. (She'd only ever seen him alone at high school.) It was all too pathetic for words – and as if to prove it, by the time they reached her home, the only noise between them was a squeaking wheel on the cart.

As they stood at her doorway – while Stephanie dug out her key – Luke felt the only thing left to say was sorry.

"Look, Steph, I'm…"

"Take my number, Shapiro. Call me some time," Stephanie said, taking out a pen and paper from her bag.

"Call you?"

"Yeah."

"You mean, like, for weed?"

"To hang out. There's no one else around. And it gets lonely in the city with no one to talk to...I think we could be friends."

Luke blinked. "Friends?"

"Sure. Friends. Pals. Homies. Whatever. Just take my number, okay? It's my own line, but sometimes all the phones ring. I don't know why. So don't be surprised if my mom or Doctor Squires picks up the phone."

She scribbled down her number and handed it to him. Luke stared at the digits, almost spellbound, as if they were written on a check.

"Okay. Great. So I'll call you..." he said, eventually looking up.

But she'd already gone.

eleven

There was something about a cleavage in summer, Luke thought. It was more than just a convergence of breasts and warmth – but also of color: the way the tan becomes darker and darker as it finally meets that black line in the center.

Stephanie smiled. "What do you want from me, Luke?" she asked.

"I, uh, I don't know," Luke said.

"Hmm...don't know? Or don't know if you want to tell me?"

The spray from the crashing ocean waves behind her spurted up to meet the white clouds above her head. For a moment there was no horizon.

"Do you want to be my friend?" she asked him. "Do you want to be my best friend? Is that what you want...? Come on, Luke. There's no one around..."

Stephanie slid one strap of her tank top from her shoulder. And then did the same thing with the strap of her bra beneath it. The tan around her cleavage became lighter as her breast moved slightly away from the other…and Luke was sure he could see the edge of a perfectly round, brown nipple peeping out from above her bra, like the crescent shape at the base of a fingernail. Or maybe it was just a shadow.

"It's okay, Luke, you can tell me what you want," Stephanie said. "After all, I'm just in your head."

It was definitely a nipple.

"Do you want to do dirty things to me?" she asked.

"No. I mean, not really," Luke said. "Not especially dirty. Just kinda…normal dirty."

Stephanie lay down, her back sinking deep into the warm dry sand.

"Do you want to fuck me?" she asked. "On the beach? In the sun? Is that 'normal dirty' enough for you?"

Luke smiled. "Maybe."

"Take your shirt off, Luke. Feel the sun on your bare skin. It's like the heat you feel from another person. This is why you crave the summer, isn't it, Luke? The sun is a lover to the lonely. But you don't have to be lonely, not any more…Touch my shoulder. Feel how warm it is…And look how short my skirt is, Luke. But you don't have to only look any more… Here."

She took his hand.

"Slide it between my thighs, Luke. Do you feel how smooth they are? Come to me, Luke…"

Luke knelt in the sand between her legs. He went to lie down on top of her.

"That's right, come to me, Luke," she told him. "Come, come, come…"

Luke's bed began to shake as he approached orgasm.

"Luke…! Luke…!"

His hand was moving up and down his cock so rapidly now that the bed head banged against the wall as quickly as a heartbeat and as loud as a knock on the door.

"Luke…! Luke…!" his dad called out again, banging on the bedroom door.

The bright sunshine; the yellow sand; the white tank top; the brown nipple – they all dissolved to be replaced by a formal black and white picture of Stephanie in the high school yearbook which was lying open on Luke's bed. (Luke's free hand was covering Doctor Squires's face.)

Fuck! It was like Battery Park all over again.

Luke pulled his underwear up and his T-shirt down, and got off the bed… He caught sight of himself in the wardrobe mirror: it looked like someone was using a pole to dispose of filthy underwear. He had to find his pants.

"Luke…! Luke…!"

"I'll be right there," Luke called out, hopping to the door as he pulled on his pants – and zipping up his flies as he unlocked it.

"What the hell were you doing in there?" his dad asked as soon as the door opened. "Did you have your headphones on?"

"Um. Yeah."

"Well, will you please turn off the air conditioner? The electric bill is through the roof."

"You think it's cooler just cuz it's night? It's ninety degrees out there."

"Then use the fan – it doesn't use as much electricity."

"The fan! The fan doesn't do anything, it just moves the warm air around."

"It's up to you, just turn the air conditioning off."

"But…"

"Just do it, Luke."

His dad turned and walked away. Luke shut the door again and gave it the finger. And then he turned the air conditioning off. He slumped back down onto his bed and looked again at the picture in the yearbook. If he was going to do it, he had to do it now, before it got too hot…

He closed the book.

His fantasies were too fake, and his reality was too real.

twelve

Luke had woken early, but his eyes were still shut tight – the way a child pretends to be asleep. It was to prevent the sweat from running into them. His hand groped along the side of his bed, searching for the T-shirt he'd worn last night. He quickly wiped his face with it and saw it was a discarded pair of boxer shorts. Disgusted, he pulled himself up onto his elbows and studied his feet in the mini-fridge, which he'd moved to the end of the bed. They were the only part of his body that was dry.

Surely it couldn't stay as hot as this for much longer. Surely the weather would break at some point. Surely it had to cool down soon...

The oscillating fan on his desk shook its head.

He got out of bed and squinted through a gap in the curtains. He could tell there was no breeze again – you did a bad fart and it followed you down the street like a stray dog – but it had to be cooler outside than it was in here.

So he quickly dressed and left his bedroom.

But as he walked through the hallway on the way to the front door, he noticed his dad in the front room. He'd opened one of the brown cardboard boxes that were littered all over the apartment and was sifting through its contents.

Luke approached him.

"So what is this stuff, Dad?" he asked.

"Walkmen. From Singapore," his dad told him, still rummaging through the box. "I got a guy who wants six thousand of these."

"That's good."

His dad looked up. "Good? It's great. Do you know how much money I stand to make?"

Luke picked up a walkman from the box, and started playing with it. "Huh. That's funny."

"What is it?" his dad asked him.

"They don't rewind."

"No?"

"I mean, there's no rewind button. Just fast forward."

His dad shrugged. "So you fast forward and flip the tape. It's the same as rewinding."

Luke pressed the fast forward button. The walkman jammed.

"This one seems broken," he said, handing it to him.

"Crap," his dad said, examining it.

Luke looked at his dad stooped over the walkman, pressing the button again and again, going nowhere

fast – until in a frenzied panic his dad started trying random walkmen; flitting from one brown cardboard box to the next, like a blue-assed fly feasting on shit.

(Luke had a horrible flashback to the time that his father invested in a patent for the "Echoless Toilet Bowl" which promised to provide "America's Most Discreet Bathroom Experience.")

"I wouldn't worry about it, Dad," Luke said, turning to leave. "Most people use CDs now anyway."

"You don't," his dad called out to him.

Luke didn't look back, as he opened the front door. "I said most people."

thirteen

The elevator pinged and the doors disappeared to
reveal two men standing side by side in the hallway.
The men were large and square and black – like the
Uzi submachine guns they were carrying. And they
stared at Luke with piercing red eyes, as if the weapons
were laser sighted.

Luke stepped out of the elevator and approached
them.

"Jesus, guys. A little dramatic, don't you think?"

The men said nothing. They just carried on staring
straight ahead.

"Is dat you, Luke?" a voice called out.

"Yeah, it's me," Luke called back to him.

"Den cum on in here."

One of the men signaled the way for Luke to go.

"I know," Luke said. "I know."

(Luke always thought that was dumb when he saw it
in movies, and seeing it in real life only made it look
dumber: if someone was pointing a gun at someone,

and they wanted that other person to move, why the fuck did they always move the barrel of the gun in the direction that they wanted that other person to go? Why didn't they just use their free hand or nod with their head? It didn't make any sense to take the gun off their target, even for a split second.)

Luke walked down the red carpeted hallway that led into what looked like a large, almost empty space. It was brightly lit with the type of highly polished wood floorboards you get in art galleries.

Or gymnasiums.

He walked over to Luke from the still swinging punch bag in the corner. He was so pumped up, even his boxing gloves seemed to have veins on them.

"Mr Luke. How you livin', boy?" he asked, trapping his right boxing glove under his left armpit and pulling his hand free.

"Barely, Percy. Barely," Luke told him.

They gave each other a fist pound.

Percy unlaced the other one and threw both gloves onto the white leather couch. Then he took an oversized Phillies Blunt T-shirt, which was hanging over the back of a chair, and threw it over his broad shoulders.

They sat down together.

"So what's with the heavy artillery?" Luke asked him.

Percy shrugged. "Guns and drugs, Luke...Don't you know? Dem go together like big white titties and brown babies."

Percy's smile was punctuated with several gold teeth.

"Seriously," Luke said.

"Seriously?" Percy said, burying the gold again. "It's dis fucking Giuliani, man. You can't be too careful. He wants to clean up da streets…I mean, what da fuck does dis Giuliani know about da streets today? Do you tink he knows what it's like to walk into a restroom and have other men's piss seepin' into your socks from da hole in da bottom of your shoe? Do you tink he knows what it's like to live in a 'hood where you're grateful it's only dog shit you stood in?"

"He's forgotten what it's like."

"Fuck, yes, he's forgot…To people like him, da ghetto is just a drowning man who will pull down anyone who tries to help."

Percy picked up a boxing glove and began to squeeze it as if it were a stress reliever.

"Don't get me wrong, Luke – a bee without a sting is just a fly," he said. "But now it's not enough to have a coupla guys with baseball caps and bats on da door. Now it's not enough to *sometimes* have to smash a bottle over somebody's head like I wuz namin' a ship. Now I gotta get mean muthafuckas with submachine guns…How da fuck is dat making da city safer?"

"It isn't, Percy."

"You damned fuckin' right it isn't!"

Percy shook his head, wiping the sweat off his forehead with his palm.

"Funny ting is, Luke, one of da guys by da elevator? I grew up with him. Remember when you wuz a kid, and you used to play dat Monopoly, and someone always says, 'I wish dis wuz real money?' Well, he wuz da kid with da toy gun who always used to say, 'I wish dis wuz a real weapon.' He said it wuz da only way of makin' da money real…I never believed dat shit, man, never. But here I am with da guns at da ready cuz dat fuckin' Giuliani declared war!"

"You're gonna shoot Giuliani?"

Percy put his finger to his lips and smiled. "Don't tell nobody."

Percy handed Luke a coke from behind the bar in another one of his large, empty rooms. Then he grabbed a remote control, pointed it at the stereo and turned up the volume.

"What is this?" Luke asked him.

"Dis is da new shit, man. I got hold of it early. It's Biggie Smalls."

Luke smiled. "It's dope."

"Dis cat is gonna change da world, man."

Percy began to pull giant bricks of weed from behind the bar, laying them on the counter, like he was lining up drinks…and like alcohol, drugs came in lots of different flavors.

"So today we have for your smoking pleasure, Mr Luke," Percy said, placing a hand on each of the bricks in turn. "Da bubble gum, da northern lights, and, of course, da purple haze."

Luke stared off into the distance.

"Everyting okay, man?" Percy asked him.

"It's nothin' ... Parental trouble."

"What about dem?"

"They're dicks."

"I tell you, man. You're a kid, and you look at your parents, at da older generation, and how dem act, and you tink, I'm never ... I am NEVER gwana do da shit dem do ... Den you grow up and do da *exact same shit*."

Luke shook his head. "No way. Not with my parents. You don't know what they're like."

"It makes no difference. A cat buries its shit with more care den I buried my old man – in fact, dey shoulda buried da fucker face down so he could see where he wuz going – but just when I tink dat he's come back to haunt me, I realize it's *me* dat's just said something dat sounds exactly like him."

Luke shook his head. "Not me."

Percy smiled. "Yes you. You'll see. Some day you gwana come in here wearing a suit and you gwana be the exact same ting dat your dad be right now ... You gwana be married to some girl like your mom and you gwana fight with her all the time ... And dat's when I'm gwana give you dis here ganja to make it all better."

"Thanks, Percy."

"Now, how much you need?"

"I could use a little bit more this time, Percy. Can you spot me?"

Percy raised an eyebrow. "You're not smokin' more cuz you're feelin' all fucked up, are you...? Cuz you remembered what your Uncle Percy told you? A dealer can't sell what he craves for himself."

"I know, Percy. I'm not using any more than usual."

"Good...how much more do you need?"

"Another five ounces."

"Hooo-boy. You got big aspirations, Luke."

"Not really. Just a lot of debt."

Percy looked at him. "You got da weight of da world on your shoulders, boy...You're not smokin' any *less*, are you? Cuz dat can be a bad ting too."

"No Percy, I'm using exactly the same – but I just need more drugs. Just this once. I'll pay you back once I unload it...Please, Percy. I'm good for it."

Percy smiled. "Just dis once, den. But you're lucky I'm so nice, boy. A lot of people in dis world ain't gwana be so nice to you."

"No shit, Percy. No shit."

Luke took the weed from Percy and put it into his backpack.

"Okay, soldier, you be careful out on da street," Percy told him, giving him a fist pound. "Dat Giuliani got dem police looking at everyting and everybody. Fuckin' Giuliani! Do you see how I am?! Da last ting a black man needs is more paranoia...! But, I tell you,

Lukey, he's even got his men checking up on white boys like you…"

"I'll be careful, Percy," Luke said, walking away. "I'm always careful."

"I know. Dat's why I like you… Hey, Luke!"

Luke turned round. Percy threw him a tape.

"It's called 'Ready to Die,'" he told him.

fourteen

"I've been thinking about your dilemma a lot recently, Luke..."

"What's my dilemma?"

"The girl thing... The fact you can't get laid."

"Well, like I said, Doctor Squires, it's not like I've *never* been laid. There was that time in Battery Park with Katie Randall and the cops and the bottles of..."

"Crazy Horse?"

"That's right, Crazy Horse. And the other thing is, if I could find a girl who would have sex with me, trust me, there would be no *dilemma.*"

Doctor Squires nodded. But the term was a professional habit with him. When faced with the choice between bad and terrible, choose bad... but which was which? That was the issue for most of the people who came into his office. When life became so dreadful, you really couldn't tell any more. Everything became a dilemma.

"You're right, Luke, it's more of a problem, isn't it?" Doctor Squires told him. "Well, I've been thinking about your problem – and the thing is, Lucas, when I went to school, if you had drugs in your top pocket, you didn't need a comb. Dealers found it easy to get girls. In fact, that's why I always wanted to be one."

"Doctor Squires, were you popular in high school?"

"Well, I wouldn't say popular, no. I wasn't one of the cool kids, if that's what you're asking. I played a little basketball…"

"Did you ever think about hanging yourself?"

"Not until much later."

"Then you must have been popular. I'm not."

Doctor Squires marveled at how sticking a ball through a metal hoop and not wanting to put his head in a noose qualified as making him popular in high school – at least in Luke's eyes.

"Well, do *you* play any sports at all, Luke?" he asked him.

"Not really. I used to be heavier when I was younger…"

Doctor Squires nodded. "It can make it difficult to play sports."

"Yeah, not getting picked for the team doesn't help, either. But I did try out for the swimming team once. I figured I weighed less in the water."

"How did that go?"

"I think I'd eaten too much before the trials. I threw up in the swimming pool. For four years I was

known as Puke Shapiro...See? Even you're smiling at that one."

"I'm sorry."

"But this is the thing – I thought that losing all that weight would help. In fact, I became more unpopular. I think the kids at school actually resented the fact that there was less of me to hate. You can only imagine how much more unpopular I'd be if I didn't deal drugs."

"Luke, this girl thing has got nothing to do with being unpopular. You're just not trying hard enough. You must think about it, Luke. Close your eyes and see it in your mind. The different scenarios: random sex in phone booths, chance encounters in discos. The way that women smell, the things that they say, even when they're saying nothing at all. Fingering them for so long, your fingertips wrinkle..."

Luke listened to Doctor Squires's guidance in amazement. It was like he was Yoda on acid...Finally, Doctor Squires's far off gaze met Luke's unblinking stare.

"I mean, I'm married, Luke," he said, "so I don't contemplate that type of thing..."

Luke nodded. "Obviously."

"Surely there's someone, Luke."

"Well, there is this one girl."

"That's fantastic, Luke. Is it Katie Randall? Is she willing to try again?"

"Um. *No.*"

"Then who is she? Does Stephanie know her?"

"Naw. She, uh, goes to school downtown."

"So what's the problem?"

"She just wants to be friends."

"What makes you think that?"

"She said so."

Doctor Squires smiled to himself. Women also tell men they want "Commitment," "Sensitivity," "Reliability"…And then they leave them for the type of men that their husbands would've been if they hadn't married their wives. Men are betrayed by themselves.

"And what makes you think that women know what they want?" he asked Luke.

"I think this one does."

Doctor Squires shrugged. "So what if she does? If we all did what we wanted, the word 'persuade' wouldn't be in the dictionary. There would be no art of seduction. *Make* her like you, Luke. That's what I did with my wife."

"How?"

(Luke mentally crossed his fingers hoping that Doctor Squires wasn't going to tell him to "just be himself," because that really wasn't a good look for him.)

"Be her friend," Doctor Squires told him. "Confide in her. Earn her trust. Then, when you are least threatening to her, grab her and stick your tongue so far down her throat that she starts to gag from pleasure."

"Can I grab her tits too?"

"Baby steps, Luke."

"Right."

"Pursue her, Luke. You're the perfect age for it. You haven't become cynical. You haven't been systematically numbed to the allure of romance. You still have your youthful…"

He started doing fist pumps.

"Okay, I got it, Doctor Squires," Luke told him.

"Young men need sex, Luke. All men, actually. Do you think your balls dropped just to get away from you…? I mean, I could get you a hooker, if you like? Two if you wanted…"

Luke looked at him. "I was this close to respecting you."

Doctor Squires took a bong hit and exhaled.

"Big mistake, Luke," he told him. "Call your girl."

"Right," Luke said, getting up to leave – but as he opened the door Doctor Squires called out to him.

"You don't need medication, Luke! You just need to get laid!"

The receptionist smirked as Luke closed the door, but Luke didn't care. All he was thinking about was how he was going to disguise his voice if Doctor Squires picked up the phone when he called Stephanie tonight.

fifteen

Doctor Squires was smoking a joint on the terrace of his penthouse; looking at the reddening skies over Central Park as dusk approached – and at the suntanned women who passed below him. Breasts were definitely getting bigger, he decided. Women used to only have tits when the sun was out. Now even sweatshirts had nipples.

Suddenly the track that was playing on the hi-fi in the living room – "Glad" by Traffic – ended. Doctor Squires turned round. He saw his wife standing there in her nightgown.

"I was listening to that," he said.

"I've got a migraine," she told him. "The pain's shooting across from one temple to the other. It's right behind my eyes. I said I was having an early night."

"Well, we just got some new pills at the office. FDA approved. You want some?"

"Please, Jeffrey. No pills, you know that."

"Fine, but a couple of pills and a scotch should fix that migraine right up. Then you could come out here

and we could watch the sunset together. It shouldn't be long now. Or are the days still getting longer?"

"They always are when you can't sleep."

She turned to go back to the bedroom.

Doctor Squires looked down at his shoes.

"Oh, Jeffrey, one more thing," she called out to him. "Please brush your teeth before you come to bed...I don't want to spend all night wondering whether the dog's got into the bedroom and farted."

"Sure."

"What?"

"Sure," Doctor Squires called back to her.

He turned round and wondered why it was in a relationship that you moved from being so interested in that other person's body, to only having the urge to report on what's going on with your own. After all, no one on a first date would ever say anything like, "I've got this really funny pain in my ear," but stuff like this is all you end up talking about when the relationship gets old. (Or, at least, this is how it seemed to be with his wife.)

He slumped his forearms back down onto the top of the ornate metal railings that ran across the terrace, and wondered whether it would give way. At least it would look like an accident. But as he looked down, in the gaps between his folded arms, he spied a young couple walking toward him hand in hand. They were smiling and looked adoringly at each other at least every few steps. They were obviously very much in love...Doctor Squires quickly reached down for one of the water bombs he kept behind a plant pot.

Sometimes he would casually lob them from the terrace, the way soldiers threw grenades in war films. Accuracy being sacrificed for esthetics (and sound effects). But not this evening. He held it with his arm high above him, waiting to drop it directly onto them. He even stood on his tiptoes so as to optimize the speed of the drop...But as they passed by, he couldn't resist throwing it down as hard as he could.

The water erupted on impact, creating, for a split second, a classic coronet shape. It would have been even more classic, Doctor Squires thought, if it had crowned their pretty little heads instead of the sidewalk. He had been, perhaps, a little too forceful. (But when they're like that, insisting on walking with their heads joined together, it was a bigger target.)

Never mind. It was fun watching them run away: he could clearly run faster than she could in heels, and a gap soon developed. (She might have something to say about that once she got her breath back.) And Doctor Squires knew there would always be another target...He just didn't think it would come along so quickly. These two were even worse, Doctor Squires decided. They were walking *arm in arm*. He dashed into the living room and came back with the phone book...and his hands soon began to shake as he held

it over the railings, it was so heavy. It was almost a relief when the phone rang.

"Hello?" Doctor Squires said.

"Oh, hi there," the voice on the other end of the line replied, in what sounded like a... *Texan accent*? "I'm looking for, um..."

"Luke?" Doctor Squires asked.

There was a long silence.

"Luke, is that you?"

"Doctor Squires?" Luke finally replied.

"It's okay, Luke. I know why you're calling."

"You do?"

"The beaver hunt."

"*The beaver –*"

"The pussy quest...I can help, Luke. Let's grab a drink. I've got just the place."

Again there was a pause as Luke tried to take everything in. He chose to be philosophical. It was all about taking baby steps, right? He had, after all, managed to find the courage to phone Stephanie's house...

"Okay," Luke agreed.

...and had succeeded in going out with her father.

Luke closed his eyes. Babies who have shit themselves don't take steps as small as this.

sixteen

"Thanks for this, Doctor Squires. I would have never have thought of coming here in the quest for pussy and the hunt for beaver. I dread to think where my inexperience might have led me…"

Doctor Squires shook his head. "I simply can't understand it, Luke. This place used to be a very popular watering hole."

"Yeah, it's like an oasis in reverse."

Doctor Squires looked around the bar. It was like a neutron bomb had gone off: everything still looked the same, except all the people were gone. (Apart from a handful of drunks.) He remembered how full of life it used to be in here. *All* of life. How you could look around and see all the different stages of a relationship happening at the same time: the pick up lines; the first kisses; the fuck in the restroom; the drinks in silence.

"The city's not the same any more, Luke," he said. "It really used to be something down here. The girls, the drugs, the music – oh, Luke, *the fucking music!* You

shoulda heard the music. Perhaps they've still got some of it…"

He went over to the jukebox in the corner. Luke stayed at the bar for a while and then reluctantly joined him…as "In the Flesh" by Blondie started up: "*Darlin'…Darlin', Darlin'.*"

"Did you hit the wrong numbers?" Luke asked him.

"No."

"This song is wack."

"Is that good?"

"No."

"Oh. Well, what kind of music do you like, Luke?"

"Tribe Called Quest. Pharcyde. De La Soul…"

"That's rap music, right? I don't know that stuff."

"I'll make you a mixtape, if you like…Or you can check it out for yourself on Stretch Armstrong's show on KCR."

"'Stretch Armstrong?' That's that toy, isn't it…? I always thought that's the perfect gift for children who won't share."

"Right. I'll make you a mixtape, Doctor Squires."

"I'd like that, Luke – but I wouldn't want you to go to any trouble."

"It's no trouble. I've never had anyone to give a mixtape to before."

Doctor Squires smiled. "Then maybe I'll make you one too," he said. "A little Bowie. A little Bruce Springsteen. Maybe some classical: Brahms, Haydn."

"Word. Haydn's dope."

"You're serious?"

Luke looked at him. "No, Doctor Squires."

They went back to their seats at the bar.

"Hey, Luke. Why couldn't Mozart find his teacher?"

"Why?"

"Because he was Haydn."

"That's not funny. Buy me another drink, please."

Doctor Squires ordered another Bud for Luke and another scotch for himself... And he stared at the ice cubes waltzing in his whiskey until Blondie's Lower East Side love story ended.

"Lucas, I hate my wife," he said.

Luke didn't look up either. "I hate my parents."

"I need to get laid."

"We both need to get laid."

Doctor Squires thought about all the sex-obsessed men that came into his office – the chronic masturbators, the serial fornicators – and how the advice that he gave in such cases of *dick-zophrenia* was always the same: "Don't womanize. Humanize. How can you be interested in the world when you only want to know half of it?" But now he wasn't too sure. Sex without love. Love without marriage. Marriage without sex. Were these the three ages of man?

"I want you to know, Luke, that I've never cheated on my wife before. Ever. But I want to now. It is my mission. You have no idea how much I want to. And

not just because I want my face buried in the stinking soaked panties of some delectable young nubile... Sometimes it's right to do the wrong things, and now is one of those times... But we gotta fix ourselves first."

"You need fixin'?" Luke asked him.

Doctor Squires looked at him. "Lucas, I need a whole lotta fixin'."

Luke reached into his pocket – when suddenly a group of loud teenagers burst into the bar. They were all dressed up in formal wear and pissed as hobos. Luke looked across at them. "Union?"

Union's head turned sharply, making her colorful dreads wrap around each other like the ribbons on a maypole.

"Oh my God – Luke!" she said, dashing toward him and giving him a hug. "I can't believe you're in here...! We dropped in to look at all the weird old people. Oh my God! Wait one second!"

She dashed off again – but Doctor Squires's tongue was still sticking out like a bookmark.

"Don't even think about it," Luke told him.

"This is the mystery girl?"

"Naw. But that don't mean she's fair game."

Still Doctor Squires couldn't take his eyes off her. "There isn't anywhere that girl could stick her finger, that I wouldn't want to lick clean..."

"Please, Doctor Squires," Luke cringed. "She might look younger than she is, but she acts younger than she looks... Why don't you just sort yourself out with a hooker?"

Doctor Squires screwed up his nose. "I like to kiss 'em, Luke. I'm a romantic at heart. What about you? Is that why you weren't interested in my offer of a hooker...? Luke?"

Luke was momentarily distracted by the idea that prostitutes never kissed their clients. Out of all the things that they did do, it was the one safe way of exchanging bodily fluids.

"No, Doctor Squires," he eventually replied. "It's just the whole idea of it. Even if I was unhappily married, I could never pay money to have sex with another woman."

"What do you think a divorce is?" Doctor Squires asked him.

Union returned with a tall, dorky looking kid dressed in a tux. He almost stumbled into them.

"Luke, this is Gruden," Union told him. "My date to the Midsummer Night Cancer Ball. It's for charity."

(Luke didn't know if she was referring to the Ball or the date.)

"The charity gave me a couple of free tickets cuz I ran the New York marathon in aid of them," Union continued. "I raised twenty-seven dollars in sponsor money."

Cancer must be shitting itself, Luke thought, as he gave Gruden a fist pound. "'Sup, Gruden?"

Union whispered to Luke, "He's an exchange student. From Rotterdam. He's a joke."

"What happened to that other dude?" Luke asked her.

"Albert? He was way immature. When I split up with him he started crying. *Physically crying.*"

Luke wondered if there was any other kind.

"Gruden, I'm Hayden," Doctor Squires said.

"Like the classical guy?" Union asked.

"Yes. I was named after him. Mother said my soul represented the metaphysical embodiment of his most sublime chord."

"That's so awesome!" Union told him, her big blue eyes becoming even bigger. "Do you like the Grateful Dead?"

"Followed them for four years after college."

Union inhaled sharply. Gruden threw up.

Luke looked around the bar's restroom and wondered how long it had been since the soap dispenser had ejaculated any soap, and the missing condom machine hadn't been merely a stencil on the otherwise nicotine stained walls. He also wondered whether Gruden had finished puking in one of the stalls yet. (Luke had reluctantly volunteered to take Gruden to the john, but the truth was, he felt sorry for Gruden. He was the Dutch equivalent of him.) Best to leave it for a little while longer, Luke thought. And he went back into the bar.

They were sitting in a booth now: Doctor Squires, Union, a couple of other kids in tuxes. Luke joined them.

"What is that thing you're rolling?" Doctor Squires asked the kid sitting opposite him.

"A blunt," the kid said.

Doctor Squires nodded. "A blunt. I like that...Where was I?"

"The second set," Union said excitedly, sitting next to him.

"Oh yes. Well, they started with 'Casey Jones,' and that's right when the acid kicked in."

Union stared at him in awe. "Amazing. I *love* the whole rock 'n' roll lifestyle thing. I wanted to join a band myself, once."

"Why didn't you?" Doctor Squires asked her.

"It was easier to take drugs than guitar lessons," she said.

Doctor Squires nodded. "Very wise."

The other kid turned to Luke. "Your dad is mad cool."

"He's not my dad," Luke told him.

"Luke is very into the rap of the Soul Tribe," Doctor Squires said. "And many of their other songs. Tell her, Luke."

Union looked at Luke expectantly, while Doctor Squires raised his eyebrows at him.

Luke's eyes flitted from one to the other. "Um..."

Doctor Squires tried to help him out. "He also likes playing the video game, 'The Prisoner of Zenda.' Does anyone else like that one?"

Now everyone looked at Luke.

"I'm just gonna see how Gruden is," Luke said, sliding out from the booth.

Being inebriated is like being in zero gravity. The slightest brush against a lamppost could send you miles in the opposite direction. And breaking wind when you urinated was the only way to stay upright.

When Luke went back into the restroom, and saw that Gruden had come out of the stall and was pissing at a urinal, he assumed that this was the only way he was managing to stand motionless. (Although Luke wondered why he didn't just use the stall, but, then again, maybe that was just Luke: he never used a urinal when he could use a stall. Not since he used a urinal last summer when he was wearing shorts, and he could feel how much urine was splashing back onto his bare legs in the form of an invisible spray – and he realized that this was happening all the time. He'd just never felt it before.)

Another guy entered the restroom and stood at a urinal next to Gruden. He shot Gruden a glance, and then looked again. "Hey Buddy," he said to him, "your dick's the one with the hole at the end of it."

Luke peered round the corner. Gruden was pointing his testicle at the urinal – actually holding it between his thumb and index finger – while his dick was going off in his pants. Luke was amazed that he could be oblivious to the warmth spreading all over his groin like a cat lying in his lap. (It was hardly an invisible spray.) He was well and truly pissed. Best to leave it for a little while longer, Luke thought. And he went back into the bar.

The kids were still at the booth, smoking weed.

But now there was no sign of Doctor Squires. Or Union.

It wasn't like they were merely kissing. It was like the music they'd been talking about was still in their heads, snake charming the tongue from the mouth of the other; making them dance, writhe, and fuck within the dark cave of their firmly pressed lips…For a moment Luke stared as open mouthed as they were, before he blinked and knocked on the phone booth door.

Doctor Squires slid it open. "The game's called 'Seven Minutes in Heaven,' Luke. Not four."

"Yeah, we still got three minutes left," Union said, checking her watch. (The stubble rash around her mouth and chin made it look like she was wearing a pink goatee.)

They went to shut the door again, but then the bartender turned up and called time on everything.

"That's enough, kids," he told them. "Y'all are too young to be in here."

"*Come on, man,*" Doctor Squires said to him. "They're all eighteen."

The bartender looked at him.

seventeen

Doctor Squires and Luke walked along the street alone.

"Since when is the drinking age twenty-one?" Doctor Squires asked him.

"Since forever."

"It's that fucking Giuliani again, isn't it?!" Doctor Squires hissed, as he looked around Times Square. "This city is a disaster, Luke. It's not even like it's New York any more. It's a theme park where the theme is New York. It's plastic. It's one big fucking Happy Meal."

"Some people like Happy Meals."

"Some people like the Yankees too, Luke. It doesn't mean they're right…Look around you. Is this what you want for your mind? For your life? You want it to become like this city? Sweep all those nasty things under the rug? Make everything okay?"

They walked on past a homeless person, sleeping in a cardboard box. Except the box was too small. His head was breaking through the top of it, and his feet

stuck out of the bottom. He looked like a child playing robots.

"He puts the homeless people in prison, Luke – you know that? These people are sick, mentally. And they're being put in jail. What do you think about that?"

Luke sometimes wondered whether we were all privately mad; it was just some people couldn't distinguish between being inside alone, and outside in public...And looking at that poor bastard lying there in the street, sharing his home with leaves and litter, it was easy to see how the failure to make this mental distinction could lead to the same physical consequences.

"It doesn't seem right, no," Luke replied.

"No. No it doesn't. And that's why I don't want you on medication, Luke. You may as well go and open a Starbucks in your brain. Do you follow me?"

"Well..."

"Don't jump at the quick fix. This whole fucking city wants a quick fix."

"Uh-huh."

"People don't lose their minds, Luke. They only lose their sense of proportion: they're not wrong to feel the things they do – only to the *extent* that they feel them. This is what we mean when we talk about an unbalanced mind...With you it's different. You're not mentally ill. There's no need to run away from your pain. Turn and embrace it, Luke. Make it a part of you. You don't want to be like them – the city and the quick fixes – thinking it's better to be synthetically happy than genuinely sad. I don't want you to be like them."

"So you've never taken that stuff?"

"Jesus, Luke I'm on all of it. But I don't want you to be like me either."

Doctor Squires stopped walking and went to urinate against a wall.

"But sex is a drug too, Luke," he said, looking down at his cock (which for once didn't feel like a worm shrivelling for lack of moisture). "And it's a drug more powerful than any synthetic pharmaceutical."

"Is that why you go around trying to fuck little girls?"

Doctor Squires's stream of urine kinked like the line of a cardiograph as it traced his laughter.

"I'm serious, Doctor Squires," Luke told him. "What did you think that looked like back there?"

"You think people were shocked by that? People *like* to see an older man with a young girl. It's like seeing a disabled person with a job. It gives everybody hope … Besides, it was just second base."

"And what happened to getting fixed first?"

"Sometimes getting laid is getting fixed, you know? Except for dogs."

He zipped himself up again.

"Now break out that blunt, Luke...Luke?"

Luke was watching the pool of Doctor Squires's urine as it made its way down the street. Fuck. Old men piss a lot! It was heading toward that homeless guy like a stream of lava. Fortunately it wasn't even a trickle by the time it got near him...but the cardboard was so dry and brittle from the heat wave that it seemed to suck it all up until it looked like the entrance to the Lincoln Tunnel. ("Fucking Giuliani!")

"Luke?" Doctor Squires said again.

"Hm?"

"The blunt...?"

"This is a joint," Luke told him, as he took it from his pocket.

"I know that."

And as Doctor Squires fumbled with his lighter, Luke passed the time by writing on the wall with a Sharpie.

Doctor Squires approached him. "Why do you do that, Luke?"

"Taggin' the wall...? I guess I'm just kinda putting my stamp on this wall. So people know I was here. In spite of everything."

"Ritualistic communication. Much like early cave painting. A crude, yet vital, form of expression."

"If you say so, Doctor Squires. All I know is this: when your back's against the wall, all you can do is write on it."

Doctor Squires wondered when graffiti became tagging; when pot became weed; and everything became, *like*, a simile. He wanted to understand young people (and their world of blunts and Sharpies). He looked at Luke's tag. He tried to interpret it like it was an ink blot. He could see rebellion in the arrows that he'd drawn on the stems of the letters. But they also resembled mini erections.

"Near to where we live, Luke – beneath one of the billboards – someone's sprayed an enormous cock on the wall. It's got hairs on the balls and five droplets of cum shooting out the end of it... Every time my wife and I drive past, we pretend not to see it."

"Well, that wasn't one of mine."

Doctor Squires smiled.

"It's illegal all this tagging, isn't it, Luke?"

"Yeah."

"I'd like to leave something on the wall, too – well, at least something that doesn't evaporate. May I...?"

"I guess," Luke said, handing him the marker pen. "Just be careful."

Doctor Squires took a deep breath and a tongue appeared at the corner of his mouth, as he neatly wrote, "Dr Jeffrey Squires, MD."

"Why don't you write down your phone number as well?" Luke asked.

Luke was about to stop him, when another voice intervened...

"Hey! You two! Stop right there!"

A couple of cops were hauling ass toward them, faster than the speed of stink. Luke looked at Doctor Squires. Doctor Squires looked at the joint in one hand and the marker pen in the other. He dropped them both – and then dropped to one knee. "It's a good thing I'm wearing these," he said.

And he began to pump up his Reebok Pumps.

Luke stared at him.

"Forrest Gump, Luke. Forrest Gump."

"What are you talking about?"

Doctor Squires looked up at him. "Running."

And he took off...

The way he'd set off from being down on one knee made it look like he was starting from the blocks. This was the only similarity to sprinting.

His urine had moved faster down the street than he did.

eighteen

The Manhattan Detention Complex was better known as the Tombs. And the large holding cell that Doctor Squires and Luke found themselves in was better described as a menagerie – crammed with an assortment of New York's illest: crackheads, domestic abusers, the homeless and the mentally sick... But throughout the night, not one of these people had made more noise than Doctor Squires.

"Who put you up to this, boys?" he asked, grabbing the bars like he was Jimmy Cagney. "Was it Giuliani? You guys got some kind of quota to fill? Used to be, you could lick a sheet of acid, hold up a bank, and fuck a whore in Times Square without you fellas batting an eyelid. Now, one blunt and we're thrown in the clink? This whole city is fucked. We give you CHARACTER!"

The cops sitting at their desks just ignored him. But this didn't stop Doctor Squires's rant.

"Everything used to be 'right on' in this city. Now it's all right wing. Politicians criticize the poor for taking

drugs, but the poor need drugs more than the rich.
They don't have houses with air conditioning and
central heating – that's if they've even got a house at all.
They sweat their balls off in the summer and they freeze
their tits off in the winter. They *need* something to
anesthetize themselves. *Fuckin' Giuliani!* You know, boys,
there was once a time when politicians acted in the best
interests of the city – *all* the city – not just the people
who voted for them. Not just the people who didn't
happen to be poor or black or homeless."

A poor, black, homeless guy tapped Doctor Squires
on the shoulder. "Man, will you shut the fuck up!"

"Come on now, brother," Doctor Squires said to
him. "Join the revolution! We float on Manhattan
Island like the crew of a merciless Captain. It is no
mutiny to take over a ship which was already ours…
What are you in here for, anyway?"

"I stabbed my wife in the pussy."

"Oh. Well…"

Doctor Squires looked at Luke, but Luke was busy
thinking about Stephanie. "Look, Doctor Squires,
maybe we should keep all this on the DL," he said.

"The DL?"

"Quiet."

Suddenly, a cop shouted through the bars:
"Squires, Shapiro. You made bail!"

Everyone in the cell cheered.

Luke felt happier with every step he took down the corridor, away from the prison cell. Until he saw what was at the end of it, and he felt like a dead man walking.

Stephanie was waiting for them, holding up a set of car keys. "Hi, Stepdaddy."

"Hi, precious," Doctor Squires said.

Luke gave a nervous nod. "Hey, Steph."

"Hey, Shapiro," she said to him. "Thanks for getting my stepfather thrown in prison. You're quite an influence."

"But…"

"It was my fault," Doctor Squires told her.

"I know," Stephanie said. "Whatcha doing now, Shapiro?"

"He's busy."

"No I'm not."

"Yes you are."

Doctor Squires and Luke both looked at each other. Stephanie looked at them both, curiously.

"Okay, Stepdaddy," she said. "How about you take the car back to the garage and I won't tell my mom about this whole little arrest thing?"

Doctor Squires stared at Luke with the mad look of a homeless man who'd just stabbed his wife in the pussy.

"Don't touch my daughter, Shapiro," he warned him.

"Stepdaughter," Luke and Stephanie replied in unison.

nineteen

Doctor Squires opened the bedroom door.

"Good morning," he said to his wife.

Mrs Squires didn't reply. She was right in the middle of her *Cindy Crawford Shape Your Body Workout* – and her limbs were blurring like Vishnu.

"Don't you want to know where I was last night?" he asked her.

"Do you want to tell me?"

"I was having an affair."

"Good for you."

"I mean, I know the most sensible way to cheat on your wife is to not tell anyone about it, but what's the point of having sex if you can't brag?"

"Quite so, Jeffrey."

She started with the jumping jacks.

Doctor Squires watched as the sweat sprayed from her head like a catherine wheel. He wished that she would stop – just for once – but he knew she wouldn't. (She was like a shark. If she stopped moving she'd drown.) He'd told her that she didn't need to lose any more weight. He'd told her that her face was getting so sucked in it looked like she'd had a vacuum cleaner nozzle shoved up her ass... Only a woman could take this as a compliment.

"Alright, I'll tell you where I really was," he said, taking a deep breath. "I was in prison, Kristen. I went to jail. I tried to outrun the cops, but they caught me."

"Perhaps if you were fitter, Jeffrey. Have you ever given any thought to exercise?"

"I'm thinking of taking these Reebok Pumps back."

"I'm serious. Wafting around a copy of the *New York Times* to get rid of the smell of cannabis does not qualify as exercise... If it did, perhaps your underwear wouldn't fit you like a swimming cap."

Doctor Squires looked down. "I go down the health club every now and then," he said.

"To use the sauna."

"Yeah..."

"You can't sweat your ass off, Jeffrey. What about the gym?"

Doctor Squires had walked *past* the gym. And he *had* looked in the window. There were women in there, wearing very little and sweating. It was always summer in a gym, Doctor Squires had thought. But what made it so appealing also made it so intimidating. (A half naked man is more vulnerable than a half naked woman. Women are used to being unfairly judged.)

He remembered venturing into a gym in the early eighties. (All the women were wearing headbands.) He'd felt so self-conscious he barely looked up – but still he could see a woman in the corner of his eye looking at him. She had a baggy green sweatshirt on, tight brown leggings and red sneakers. He was doing bicep curls for ten minutes before he realized she was a tall shrub in a plant pot.

"Perhaps I could take up basketball again," he said. "I used to play it in high school, you know."

"Yeah, but you were taller then…"

Doctor Squires shook his head. "Kristen, I don't know how we've got on to the state of my ass and how far it is off the ground. I've just told you that I've spent the night in jail…Don't you care at all?"

His wife didn't reply. She'd started with the high kicks. It looked like she was goosestepping.

twenty

Luke and Stephanie strolled along the beautiful East Village street. Luke had never been on bail before. It felt good.

"So what's the deal with you and my stepdad?" Stephanie asked. "Are you guys, like, gay together?"

Luke looked at her. "We weren't in prison for that long, Steph."

"So what is it then? Some kind of surrogate father–son thing?"

Luke thought about their relationship. He could certainly see the advantages of having a surrogate father – even if you had a biological father that you really got on well with. The problem with real dads, as far as Luke could see, was that any advice they gave you was tainted by the fact that you assumed they applied it to your mother – which meant they didn't really talk about anything important at all. (Certainly not the sort of things that were important to a seventeen-year-old.) Nonetheless, the relationship

still didn't feel that way between himself and Doctor Squires.

"We're friends, I guess," Luke said.

Despite the soaring temperature, Stephanie shivered. "*Weird.*"

"Not really," Luke told her. "He's very immature."

"You could say that... It's ironic, really. Mom does everything she can to stay looking young – but she hates the fact that Doctor Squires refuses to grow up. They fight about it all the time."

"I know. We got more in common than you think, Steph."

"Your parents too?"

"Yeah... Do you think that divorce is the answer?"

Stephanie shrugged. "Divorce is to marriage what chemotherapy is to cancer: it might get the job done, but it's never gonna be pretty."

They carried on walking in silence for a while.

"You know he can't help it," Luke said. "Doctor Squires, I mean."

Stephanie smiled. "I know. Don't tell him, but I actually find his behavior kind of funny... In a ridiculous kind of way."

"Your secret's safe... So what do you wanna do today, Steph?"

"Why don't you get your cart and we go to the Park again – but not to sell anything this time."

Luke was crouching at the water's edge.

"What are you trying to do?" Stephanie asked him.

"Find my reflection."

"It's not in there."

"No shit. This water's mad dirty."

Luke got to his feet – just as the warm breeze which had been prodding the Lower Pond momentarily relented … and the smooth gray water briefly reflected the bright sky, like the wet slates of rooftops after a shower.

"You got great timing, Shapiro," Stephanie said.

Luke shrugged. "I know."

He walked back up the gentle incline to where Stephanie was sitting within the tassels of the unmowed grass, eating an ice cream beneath the shade of a tree. It was the perfect summer scene – except, as Luke sat down next to her, he could see there was still spring blossom on the ground – buried within the long green strands – but it was no longer entirely pink and white. The edges had started to turn brown and crinkle. Luke held some in his hand. The middle of summer was fall for blossom, he thought.

Stephanie turned to him. "So, why did we never hang out in high school?"

"Cuz I was a loser, I guess. Not a loser, really. I was the most popular of the unpopular …"

"Or the most unpopular of the popular."

"Right. Either way you're out of my league."

"So I'm slumming now?"

"You could say that…"

"You know, Shapiro, this whole 'popularity' thing…Friendships are like relationships. If they were both as good as they were meant to be, we would have fidelity and we wouldn't need more than one friend. Everyone surrounds themselves with people because they have to."

"Not everyone…Want a brew?"

"Sure."

He went to the cart, which they'd loaded with ice cream and beers. (It was the closest Luke had ever come to having a picnic.) And he pressed play on the boombox while he was there…Biggie started with "Everyday Struggle."

"Who is this?" Stephanie asked, as Luke handed her a bottle.

"Notorious B.I.G. Real dope."

"You should make me a mix some time."

"Definitely."

Luke pulled a joint out from his pocket and lit it. "Wanna smoke?" he asked her.

"Okay," she said.

And they passed the joint to one another and looked out over the pond – as the breeze scattered the sun across the rippling dark water like a million stars – but occasionally they caught each other's eye, and quickly glanced away.

By the time the joint and Biggie was half over, Stephanie was high on the weed, and Luke was high on her saliva.

"It's kind of nice. With no one else around," Luke said.

"You mean no one else being around the pond? Or everyone from high school being away for the summer?"

"Both, I guess."

Stephanie looked at him. "It is, isn't it?"

Luke quickly leant over and kissed her on the lips. Stephanie instinctively pushed him away. "What are you doing?" she asked him.

"Nothin'," Luke said.

"You got great timing, Shapiro."

Luke shrugged. "But did it feel good?"

"What is this, Shapiro? Kiss first and ask questions later?"

"You still haven't answered my question."

Stephanie thought for a while.

"Let's try again," she said.

There was nothing hasty about it this time. A series of small, closed-mouthed kisses ensued. But like the final hops of a pebble as it skimmed across a pond, they became tighter and faster until, at last, they succumbed to wetness.

Stephanie's soft lips felt even softer to Luke as she moved them apart. And for once he could taste the

beer and the weed together, not one after the other. It fused with the smell of the sunshine which simultaneously mixed with the sound of the hip hop. And it all combined in Luke's brain to create a new narcotic more addictive than crack. (*High Summer*, Luke would call it.)

But just when he thought the hit couldn't get any better, "Everyday Struggle" – an ode to death and drug dealing – faded out... and Biggie's magnum opus of love began: "Me and My Bitch."

They were well into the third verse by the time they pulled away from each other again. Stephanie took a deep breath.

"*Weird*," she said.

"But did it feel good?"

Stephanie smiled.

And Luke knew that because of this moment, no matter what happened, he was going to be buying whatever Biggie did for the rest of his life.

twenty-one

Doctor Squires stopped at the bedroom door, which was slightly ajar. He could see his wife in bed with a sleep mask on. He thought she looked like a cartoon burglar – having stolen away from him for yet another early night. But it wasn't migraine this time. It was exhaustion from another Cindy Crawford workout. (This was in addition to the one she'd done earlier that day.) Doctor Squires was convinced she'd only done this second session to try to make him feel guilty about not exercising at all. Fuck it, he thought. Women have to perform all these routines to keep looking young, but there was only one exercise that men had to do: clasp their left hand firmly with their right; bend their knees; and pray to God they don't go bald.

He took a modicum of comfort from running his fingers through his shoulder length hair...But as he carried on tiptoeing down the hallway on his way to the bathroom, he became aware that he was now past that age where it was possible to walk completely silently: his

knees were talking to each other like a pair of dolphins. And he remembered how, when he got up from the couch at the end of the night, it was as if he were trying to stand up on stilts. And when he got out of bed in the morning, he had to help his legs into his underwear like he was helping a child into a pushchair.

He entered the bathroom and looked at himself in the mirror. He wondered whether this was why they called them the "fall years:" because your hair changed color like the leaves, and you shortened like the days. And he looked at what he was wearing. They say past a certain age a man should stop wearing jeans, but maybe he should abandon the polar necks as well – it was getting too *busy* above the high collar. (He could see the beginnings of testicular jowls.)

He turned away from himself and sat down on the toilet. But it only reminded him that now, when he took a piss, he had to push – and when he wiped his ass, making his cock wobble, droplets of urine fell from the end of it and landed on his pants around his ankles. He was clearly having trouble turning the tap on *and* off. How infirm was that? (Jesus! When he farted in a chair he had to raise a leg like a peeing dog to help it out.)

Oh, fuck this.

He shot up, opened the medicine cabinet and took out the bottle of lithium. And despite the onset of arthritis (which was obviously why he was now struggling with the child lock), he succeeded in getting the lid off. Of course, he had no choice. He *needed* what was inside that bottle. He was very depressed.

And very sad.

Suddenly, he remembered everything he'd told Luke.

He tapped the bottle and a pill tumbled into his palm. He tapped it again. And again. And again. Finally, he emptied the entire contents into his hand... and poured them into the toilet.

When he entered the living room, Doctor Squires was surprised to find Stephanie there. She was eating ice cream, smoking a cigarette, watching *Three's Company*.

"Aren't you going out again?" he asked her.

"Not tonight."

"Did you have a nice day with Luke?"

"What do you mean?"

"Nothing... Do you like him?"

"I don't know. What do you care?"

"Do you *like* like him?"

"Maybe. Yeah."

Doctor Squires's face dropped.

"He's a drug dealer," he told her.

Stephanie looked at him. "Uh, yeah. I know he's a drug dealer. *We both buy drugs from him...* Look, I'm not really in the mood for a stepfather–stepdaughter moment, Doctor Squires."

"Well, can I watch TV with you?"

"Whatever."

"Cool."

He sat down next to her. Jesus Christ jumped up onto his lap. (It was different for animals, Doctor Squires thought. As they got older they didn't lose their looks and repulse people.)

"So," Doctor Squires said. "How 'bout you fill me in."

"Well, there's been a big misunderstanding, and Mr Ferley thinks Jack's gay."

Doctor Squires lit a joint.

"I think I've seen this one," he said.

twenty-two

"Can I make you something for breakfast, honey?"
Luke's mom asked him when he walked into the
kitchen the next morning.

"Absolutely," Luke replied.

She turned round. "Really?"

"I mean, yeah, what do we have?"

"Some fruit. Some leftover stuffing. Some bagels."

"That's fine."

"What?"

"Just put some stuffing on a bagel, please ... With
some fruit on top."

"Uh-huh ..."

She looked at him curiously as she went to get a plate.

"We never saw you last night," she said. "You went
straight up to your room. Is everything okay?"

Luke knew it would freak his parents out if they saw
him happy for once, so he'd gone upstairs to put a lid
on his emotions – and to smell Stephanie on his clothes,
while he listened to Biggie.

"Everything's fine, Mom. It was late, that's all."

"It wasn't that late."

Well, it was certainly dusk by the time he'd walked Stephanie back home. He remembered long shadows from the trees and the lampposts marking the road like a barcode...and after he'd kissed Stephanie good-bye, he remembered the sidewalk illuminating, paving stone after paving stone, as he danced over it like Michael Jackson in the "Billie Jean" video.

"Honestly, Mom, everything's fine...In fact, I think I'm in love."

His mom whipped round; a ball of stuffing flew across the kitchen like a dirty snowball.

"Luke! That's wonderful! Who's the lucky girl?"

"Stephanie Squires."

Luke said the words again in his head. He liked alliteration.

"Her family's very wealthy, Luke."

"I know."

"Well, that's good."

"It's not like we're getting married, Mom."

"You never know. This is around the time when I met your father..."

Luke winced. "Right."

(When dealing with parents, Luke decided, lids on emotions should really come with child locks.)

He escaped into the living room. His dad was sitting on the couch looking at a letter. He didn't look up as Luke entered. It was undoubtedly another bill. They woke up every morning to the sound of them: the plastic window on the front of the brown envelopes crackled like train station toilet paper as they were squeezed through the letterbox like turds...But this one was different. His dad wasn't reading it – his eyes weren't moving – he was just staring at it.

"What's that?" Luke asked him.

"Hm...? Oh, it's nothing."

Luke snatched it from him and read it. "*We're getting evicted...?*"

"Keep your voice down," his dad hissed, snatching the notice back from Luke's hand. "I'll take care of it. I've got a big deal coming through. It's no problem."

"Where would we go?"

"I don't know. Downtown maybe? Jersey? Not everyone has to live on the Upper East Side."

Jersey...? The stuff of life was now a life of stuff. Luke, however, didn't care about such things; he was always prepared to make material sacrifices – but his life was in Manhattan.

"Well, I can't live in Jersey," he told his dad.

"Look, I messed up. But I'm trying to fix it."

"Well, fix it."

His dad shook his head. "If I rip open my shirt, Luke, you won't find a big red 'S' there – only chest

hair going gray. All I can do is try. That's all any man can do."

"Then be a man, Dad. And fix it."

"What should I do, Luke? Sell pot?"

Luke looked around at all the boxes of lame walkmen. "I don't think you'd be very good at that."

twenty-three

Using the holes in the margin of his notepad as the center of flowers, Doctor Squires drew petals around them. And colored each one black.

"So, I'm having to deal a lot more now..." Luke told him.

"Uh-huh," Doctor Squires said, moving over to his prescription pad to doodle Christmas trees without decorations.

"Cuz I'm trying to help my folks out, you know. I'm just feeling a lot of pressure..."

"You're totally wrong for each other."

"Huh?"

"I want you to stop seeing Stephanie. She is not for you."

Luke looked at him. "Let me get this straight. You're happy that Stephanie buys drugs from me, but not that she spends time in my company...You do know that I come here to try to feel better about myself, don't you?"

"She'll break your heart, Luke. She's just bored."

It was hard to say which of these statements hurt Luke the most: the bullets were of the same caliber.

"That's not true," Luke told him.

"Fine. Ignore my advice. I'm trying to help you, Shapiro. What? You think she's hot? You want to fuck her? The next thing you know, you've wasted your entire life on a girl you have nothing in common with."

"Actually, I was following your advice, Doctor Squires. Living, remember? And you seemed to think then it wasn't such a bad thing to get my heart broken."

"That was a mistake, Luke. I was wrong to say that. There is nothing to be gained from having your heart broken. In time, your memory of such events might fade – but never your reaction to them. That's what will always haunt you: the realization that you were so easily capable of being destroyed."

"And what about the living? Were you wrong about that too? Anyway, what did you mean when you said about wasting my entire life? Who said anything about my entire life?"

"This is it, Luke. This is your life. The choices you make. And I guess you've chosen to be a hoodlum drug dealer, who…"

Luke blinked. "'*A hoodlum drug dealer*?' I deal some weed, and now I'm Scarface…?"

Doctor Squires looked him up and down. "You think I don't know you, Shapiro? You think I haven't had an unbroken line of dealers that go right back to the seventies? Only the fashions change. You're a hoodlum drug dealer who latches onto the only girl who will pay attention to him, simply because he's afraid of being alone."

"What about you?"

"What about me?"

"Telling me not to take medication. Your '*you don't want to be like Times Square*' fucking metaphor. You said so, you're on half that shit yourself. You're a hypocrite... Why are you even hanging out with me anyway? Don't you have friends your own age? Don't you feel like a weird old idiot, just, like, trying to relive your high school years cuz you fucked them up the first time?"

"Hey, Luke. I had your years. There's no guarantee you'll have mine."

"I wouldn't want them – going round trying to fuck little girls because you think it'll make your dick look bigger... Maybe that's it. Maybe that's what this is all about. Maybe you're jealous..."

"Don't, Luke..."

"Of me and your daughter..."

The hair around Doctor Squires's top and bottom lips knitted together as his jaw tightened.

"Stepdaughter," he corrected him. "And I believe our time is up."

Luke looked at him equally focussed.

"I guess so," he said.

"That was a short one, so I'll just charge you a dime bag."

Luke went into his backpack and pulled out a bag of weed, and handed it over with something else he'd taken from his pocket.

"I made that for you," Luke told him, as he left. "It's a mixtape."

twenty-four

Doctor Squires had sometimes seen rap videos on MTV in Stephanie's room. They always seemed to feature some guy wearing pimpwear – a long coat, a floppy hat – with a young, often scantily clad, female companion. It reminded him of watching *Doctor Who* on PBS. But listening to Luke's mixtape on the terrace – without being distracted by any images – he'd found empathy in the lyrics: the street poetry; the urban philosophy; the sentiments of hurt, anger, and despair.

(He also found the rhythm most conducive to throwing water bombs.)

Inspired, he went inside to see whether he, too, could exorcize such feelings that were particularly deep inside of himself today…

When Mrs Squires came home, she was surprised to find her husband sitting naked on the bed. With his legs crossed. Playing the guitar.

"You're home early," she said, looking at her watch.

He stopped playing. Or rather, he abandoned his search for a doleful chord. Or indeed, any chord.

"My last patient canceled," he told her. "Actually, he killed himself yesterday. Anyway, here I am."

"Oh."

There was a long pause as Mrs Squires seemed to be considering whether there was any need to say anything further. And if so, what exactly?

"Was it ... sudden?" she asked him.

Doctor Squires looked at her. "He killed himself, Kristen."

"I mean, sudden in the way of unexpected."

"It's always a risk, of course, but it wasn't like I'd only pencil in his appointments or anything ..."

"So you didn't know that he was considering suicide?"

Doctor Squires considered the question. He remembered the patient once telling him that he had thought about killing himself – but he couldn't bear the idea of his life flashing before his eyes just as he died. (Did that mean he *was* considering suicide? Or that he'd ruled against it?)

"I don't know, Kristen ... but I knew he was a Catholic."

"So?"

"The Catholic Church discourages all forms of independence – drugs, masturbation, suicide. It doesn't like people doing anything to themselves."

Doctor Squires had always suspected that Christ was crucified because it's one of the few methods of killing someone which is impossible for someone to do alone (it's the third nail that's the problem). There had to be no possibility that history could record the death as self-inflicted.

"And I knew he took his religion seriously," Doctor Squires continued. "He told me he'd considered the priesthood when he was younger. He said it seemed like a pretty powerful job – even though people were always going to go above your head and pray to God directly."

"Well, there you go, Jeffrey. If you knew he believed in these things, then you weren't to know he would do it."

She went to leave – and her husband went back to playing the guitar as tunefully as an egg-slicer – but she stopped at the bedroom door.

"Is that all that's bothering you today, Jeffrey?" she asked him. "Life, death, God, and the universe? Or is there anything else?"

He stopped playing again.

"Kristen. Do you think I'm old and weird?"

She turned round. "What?"

"I mean, they say forty is the new thirty. So fifty is…"

"No, fifty's fifty. It's old."

"I'm being serious."

"So am I."

What did he expect? His wife denied she was approaching middle age by claiming she intended to live longer than most people. But hadn't he also been in denial? He'd always been so child-like that now – faced with the mounting evidence of his advancing years – he seemed to have gone from young to old with nothing in between. It was like waking up from a coma.

"I don't know what you're worrying about, Jeffrey," his wife said, in a rare mix of confusion and compassion. "I'm sure there are plenty of younger men who would love to look like you at your age."

"I don't want to look like me at my age. I want to look like me at their age. Do you think Death counts your wrinkles and the hairs on your head? He's not going to pass you by because you *look* okay. He counts your years – and I'm getting too many."

"I don't understand. I thought you had a death wish anyway?"

"I did. I do. It's just. It's different when you don't have the choice."

"Oh. I see."

"And what about the weird?"

Mrs Squires thought for a while.

"I would definitely say you have an undiagnosed personality, Jeffrey."

"Isn't that the same as being weird?"

"Yes."

137

Doctor Squires shook his head and smiled.

"Kristen, do you...? You don't love me any more, do you?"

His wife sat down next to him on the bed. She shrugged sadly.

He closed his eyes. He'd known this for a long time, and yet there had always been hope – like in the morning, when she turned toward him half-asleep... then she turned away again. He'd told himself it was just his breath.

"It's okay. I don't blame you. I'm a mess," he said.

"You've always been a mess."

"But we used to be a mess together. We were a beautiful mess. Can't you remember when we used to walk down the street together? No one could tell who was holding who up."

"You can't be a mess forever... Sometimes you have to clean the mess up."

She ran a finger across his back like she was checking for dust.

"Okay. I'm sick of the mess metaphor," he said.

Mrs Squires laughed in spite of herself... Then she sighed.

"You see?" Doctor Squires said to her. "The way you sighed then, like you'd just blown your diet. When did you lose your sense of humor, Kristen?"

"I didn't. Life stole it."

"I can still see the traces of a smile."

"Are you still taking your pills?"

"I don't need pills. Not those pills, anyway."

They stared at each other for a short while, which for them was a long time.

"What if we went somewhere?" Doctor Squires asked. "Got out of the city for a while. We could go back to Barbados, if you like."

"I thought you were scared of flying?"

"Technically, it's the crashing that I'm afraid of. Nonetheless, would you like to go?"

"I might like that. Sure."

"We could make it an early anniversary present to ourselves. Unless you would rather do something different for our anniversary…"

"You mean, other than hold the usual three minute silence?"

"I thought you'd lost your sense of humor, Kristen."

"Who says I'm joking?"

"Alright, then let's call it a second honeymoon."

"We never had a first one."

"Then it's agreed."

twenty-five

They'd gone back to the Lower Pond again – except Biggie wasn't playing on the boombox this time. It was "Reminisce" by Mary J. Blige. And they'd gone back much further.

"He OD'd when I was six," Stephanie said. "At least that's the story they tell me. He was this very handsome, like, famous photographer, and my mom was a model. They gave me very good genes…And very bad habits. But then again, it wasn't like the drugs had ever got in the way of his work. Apparently, even when he got the shakes, he could get away with it. But I guess you can't fix your life to a tripod, can you?"

"You miss him?" Luke asked.

"I didn't know him well enough to miss him. But I'm definitely missing something…My mom had a real hard time when he died. She started to drink heavily."

"That must've been bad."

"Well, it wasn't like *Arthur*, that's for sure."

"No. Of course."

"But she managed to kick it, eventually."

"That's good."

"Then she started with the hard drugs."

"Oh."

"She was in and out of rehab. I mean she's clean now. And she's very philosophical about it. She says she'd rather be addicted to heroin than French fries – cuz the drugs, they never got in the way of her work either, you see. It was all bee-stung lips and tits. It only made it easier to keep the weight off. Then again, she was always skinny, even before..."

Her voice trailed off as she leant back onto her elbows, watching the smoke from their shared joint float across the grass like pollen.

"You know, it's weird," she said. "I've seen all the old photos of her, and she always looks the same. 'If in doubt, pout,' she always said. But I can always tell the pictures that my dad took – and it's got nothing to do with his individual style: a photo isn't just what my dad saw when he looked at her, you see. It's also an image of her looking back at him. There was something in her eyes. It's not there any more."

Luke wanted to put his arm around her and gently kiss her hair at the warm parting. (He wondered why this would be considered more intimate than sticking his tongue down her throat.)

"You okay?" he asked her.

"I'm okay," she said. "It's just sometimes I get to thinking – I look so much more like my mom, you see – and sometimes I wonder, if I looked more like him, would it be of some comfort to her when she looked at me? Or would it only make it worse?"

"I'm sure your mom wouldn't change you for the world, Steph."

Stephanie smiled.

"Well, when I get to college I think I'm gonna change my name to Mary J. Squires," she said.

"That's cool. I like that."

"Hey, what are you doing this weekend?"

"Nothing."

"Good. My folks are going to Barbados, which means my beach house in Fire Island is open. I was wondering if you wanted to join me out there for some beachcombing."

"Like, a date?"

"Like a honeymoon."

"I do."

She turned to face him. "You know what people do on a honeymoon. Don't you, Luke?"

She raised an eyebrow theatrically.

"I think so," Luke said, smiling.

They pulled themselves up to their feet and brushed themselves with their hands. The dry grass and fine dust floated upwards in the warm air – and

the barely pink and white blossom fell from them like old confetti.

Luke went to push the cart, but Stephanie stood in front of it.

Luke's shoulders slumped. "Not again?"

She looked up at him. "*Please.*"

"Oh... Alright then."

Luke gripped the wooden handles of the cart as hard as his moist palms would allow and ran along the path with it as fast as his weed filled lungs would let him; while Stephanie clung to the front of the cart, kicking her legs in the air, laughing and screaming like she was six years old again.

twenty-six

Luke placed his tongue firmly against his lower teeth –
to imitate the hiss of steam – as he waited for the sun
to lower itself into the Atlantic Ocean. This is how
much of a novelty it was to him. He couldn't, after all,
remember the last time he'd been out of the city; the
last time he hadn't seen the sun disappear behind
rooftops or tall trees. (The days were shorter in the
city, he thought.) He took a deep breath and perched
forward in the sand, as if the extra few inches would
enable him to see the sun better, as it finally approached
the horizon...when Stephanie called out to him from
the porch of her beach house.

"Want some wine, Shapiro?"

Luke turned round.

"Got anything stronger?" he called back, as if to
compensate for the embarrassment he now felt at his
private immaturity.

"I dunno. I'll just go and check through the
cabinets."

Thirty seconds later.

"What about whiskey?" she asked.

Whiskey? Luke wondered whether that was the same as scotch. It made little difference. He'd tried neither.

"That fine," he said. "Anything to mix it with?"

"There's some juice boxes…"

"Good."

Stephanie disappeared back into the house, and Luke was about to turn toward the ocean again, when he noticed how long his shadow had become. It was almost touching the white picket fence. He couldn't remember seeing his shadow this long before…but, then again, he couldn't remember ever seeing the sun this low before either. His shadow was now at its optimum length.

Unless…

He quickly turned back to the ocean before he succumbed to the equally immature temptation to see how long his shadow would be if he were standing up. With his arms above his head. He reminded himself he was about to drink whiskey. And juice.

He was sure horizons weren't meant to slope. Wouldn't it make the water sloosh to one side? He buried his fingers deep into the darkening sand to remain sitting upright.

"This whiskey is a lot of drunk," Luke said.

Stephanie looked at him. "No shit."

"So, listen, let me ask you something…" he said, looking away from the confusing water.

"Uh-oh."

"Um, what's going on here?"

"What do you mean…? Is this, like, a girlie conversation?"

"Maybe. Sorry. I mean, I've just never really been in this situation before."

"What situation?"

"Hanging out with a girl who likes me…who I like…Oh, I almost forgot." He leant over to the boombox and stuck in a tape he'd pulled from his pocket. "I made this for you."

"Slow Down" by Mary J. Blige gently undulated between the sounds of the waves.

Stephanie smiled.

"I guess I'm just wondering…" Luke continued. "What happens…when everyone comes back."

"Like, do I turn into a pumpkin?"

"Basically, yeah."

"What does it matter what's *going* to happen?"

"I wish it didn't matter. But it does. It's like before – when I was waiting for you to come out with the drinks – I was looking at the mad shadows. And I was thinking how a shadow reminds us of how things will look without the sun. Even when you're standing in the brightest sunshine, a cloud is always clipping at your heels; warning you not to get too comfortable…And I

looked at the seagulls flying and I thought, yeah, that's
the most distinctive thing about being a bird. Being
free of your own shadow. Because we're always
attached to them."

"Hm. I always thought the most distinctive thing
about being a bird was that they did white shit. Can
you think of any other creature that does white shit?"

She started to laugh.

"I'm being serious, Steph."

"I know you are, Luke, and that's the whole
problem... Shapiro, you just – you think about things
in this shitty way, you know. I'm lucky. I'm not like you.
I look at the dopeness. And you – you look at the
wackness."

"I do?"

"You do. When all you have to do is look at me."

"Word."

"And kiss me..."

It was like their very first kiss in the Park all over again.
Except now they were lying on the bed in the beach
house... in their underwear... and it was Stephanie
who was sticking her tongue down Luke's throat.

Luke wondered whether Doctor Squires had ever
had a conversation with Stephanie similar to the one
with him... But if he had, there had clearly been no
mention of baby steps: she'd pulled down Luke's
underwear like it was a reverse wedgie and, just as

quickly, she'd removed her own. Luke had thought of
trying to look at her vagina – but before he knew it, his
head was forced back again onto the pillow and she
was kissing him all over the face and neck, panting in
his ear. Foreplay is like starting a fire, Luke thought.
Heavy breathing encourages the flame.

Except this was barely foreplay.

Luke looked on helplessly as she straddled him. He
thought she would at least remove her bra next but she
went straight to taking hold of the end of his cock and
moving it up and down the length of her slit like it was
eeny, meeny, miny, moe, until it stopped at the entrance
of her vagina.

"Condom…? Condom…?" Luke said, in a state of
panic.

"That's what the pill's for, Shapiro," she said,
lowering herself down onto him and swallowing his dick.

She started moving sensuously up and down on his
cock and occasionally swaying from side to side – as if
she were dancing with it, because when the music on
the boombox started to fade ("Passin' Me By" by The
Pharcyde), so did she.

She looked down. "Um, you're not hard."

Luke looked shocked. "Fuck. No? Man…Actually,
to be honest, I think it's the booze. I never knew
whiskey was that strong. I'm really drunk. I think."

Actually, to be honest, he was also really intimidated
– and it didn't make any sense to him. All those

times, in his bedroom, Luke only had to think of
Stephanie and his dick had straightened like a tow
rope, yanking his balls away from his asshole like a
double-barreled sling shot... But now, when she
wasn't merely in his mind but he was, in fact, inside
of her, the exact reverse. (Luke was sure one of his
balls would've ended up inside his asshole if they
both hadn't tried to hide in there at the same time.)

At least the music stopping had given him the
excuse to move.

"I gotta flip the tape," he said.

"Nuh-huh. We're having sex."

"But... my drunk. I mean, my dick."

"I'll make some coffee."

Stephanie uncoupled herself from him – it wasn't
difficult – and disappeared into the kitchen. Luke
placed his forearm across his forehead and stared up
at the ceiling. He thought about how he would
normally spend his Friday nights – playing "The
Legend of Zelda." At least the shame was private...
But then again, maybe a defective dick was like a
Nintendo cartridge: if it doesn't work, blow on it and
reinsert.

They sat on the edge of the bed wearing Doctor and
Mrs Squires's bathrobes, staring into their cups in
silence.

"I never drank coffee before," Luke told her.

"I drink it all the time," Stephanie said. "It's like Ritalin."

"Hey, Steph…Not to be, like, a bitch or nothin', but, um…"

"What is it?"

"I've kinda never had sex before."

Stephanie looked at him. "*You're a virgin?*"

"Nah…I've just…never officially had sex."

"Right…I thought you fucked Katie Randall."

"I was, like, real faded and I never really – it was more like third base…"

"She thinks you fucked her."

"Well, okay, but, listen, that's why I'm nervous and, like, maybe that's why – the thing with my dick…"

Stephanie shook her head. "It's a lot to take in."

"Yeah. I know. I didn't mean to faze you."

"Not for me. For you: whiskey, coffee, sex…Well, don't worry, Shapiro. I've had sex, like, a hundred times. I'll teach you. You will be my student of sex."

Luke smiled. "Okay. I'm down."

"Yeah. But are you up for it?"

"Hm?"

"Are you sober yet?"

Luke looked at his crotch.

"Probably," he said.

"Then it's time for our first lesson."

Stephanie had promised to be gentle. The candles that she'd lit cast a light more subdued than the final embers of dusk. And she turned the volume on the boombox really low ("One Love" by Nas had just kicked in), so Luke could hear what she was whispering in his ear.

"Okay. Now put it in … Ow. Ow … Slowly. Slower … Okay. That's good. Now move in and …"

Luke shuddered. She stopped whispering.

"No fucking way," she said.

"Um …"

"You came?"

"Uhhhh …"

"You fucking came."

Stephanie shook her head as the first drop of wax ran down a candle's stem.

"Jesus, Shapiro," she said. "You can dunk a cookie into a cup of coffee more times than that."

Luke began to convulse again.

"Are you crying now?" she asked him.

"Yes," Luke sobbed.

twenty-seven

The next morning Luke was sitting on the beach watching Stephanie in the sea. He didn't feel like swimming. In fact, he didn't feel like doing anything. Stephanie had told him to forget about it, but how could he? They say you always remember your first time. What a terrifying thought. First, he couldn't get a hard on, and then he came. Wasn't there meant to be something in between...? Jesus. His sperm must have been swimming in whatever they'd brought with them last night. Stephanie must have been barely damp.

He covered his face with his hands and audibly groaned. First Katie Randall, now Stephanie: both thought he'd fucked them, but neither could be entirely sure.

The only difference was he didn't care what Katie Randall thought...

He looked at Stephanie through his fingers, lying on her back in the water; her hair splayed and floating around her beautiful face like a dark halo.

"I love you," he thought.

But she couldn't hear him, half submerged like that – and Luke began to wonder what it would be like to say the words out loud, when Stephanie was at least there, and not just in her yearbook. So...

"Steph, I love you," he said.

"I love you, Stephanie Squires," he said even louder.

Until finally...

"I got mad love for you, shorty. You make me wanna listen to Boyz II Men."

He sighed. There was nothing else he could do. He got to his feet and trudged back to the beach house, to reluctantly wash her scent from him.

The water from the outside shower pounded onto the concrete with the same deafening ferocity as rain hitting the sidewalk during a storm. Luke's eyes were closed. The first he knew that Stephanie had joined him was when he felt her fingers within his, also rubbing the shampoo into his hair.

He smiled for the first time that day. It felt good. He let his arms drop to his sides.

It surprised him how strong Stephanie was for someone so slight. He could feel each of her fingers pushing deep into his scalp – pulsating – as they drew closer and apart. (He could imagine the movement of her hands in the water. They looked like jellyfish swimming.) Then Stephanie raised her fingers onto their tips, and retraced her movements with her manicured nails. Luke's shoulders rose up to his ears as she touched the nape of his neck, and he could feel the tingle of soapy water as it began to run down his urethra...

Perhaps it was just as well she was behind him.

But she turned him round to rinse the soap from his eyes and when he opened them, he could see that Stephanie, too, was naked. Her breasts were as brown as her nipples, and her nipples were as erect as his cock. She kissed Luke gently – and went again to guide him... but now his cock was guiding Luke. He pushed Stephanie back against the wooden shower door and she wrapped a leg around him as he entered her.

At first, with each push, he was understandably nervous. But like a boxing referee, he stopped counting at ten... And in the end, Luke didn't know how long he managed. All he could remember was, when he entered Stephanie, the water was bouncing off his shoulders to create a sunlight drenched spray that began to mix imperceptibly with the rising steam... and by the time he came, there was no horizon.

Luke was suddenly reminded of all those times he'd been fantasizing over Stephanie, and he wondered how he could have masturbated in such detail over something he'd never done – but which had turned out to be almost exactly like this... So why

shouldn't it end the same way as it had on all those other occasions?

"I love you, Steph," he said.

And even though Stephanie's back was still firmly against the wooden door, she still managed to retreat.

"Whoa, dude," she said.

That wasn't how it ended, Luke thought.

twenty-eight

Doctor Squires was sitting on the terrace of their
Barbados hotel room, looking down at the hotel
pool. He was thinking about the way people came
out of pools in movies. They hardly ever used a
towel. They almost always stuck a bathrobe on. It
always looked uncomfortable to him. But maybe
that's why people like the movies. They're not like
real life.

His wife joined him with a couple of glasses and a
bottle of champagne in a bucket of ice that they'd
ordered for breakfast. She tried to clear a space on
the table, which was covered with a mess of dirty
glasses and spilled pills from the night before. She
soon gave up. They drank from the bottle and passed
it between them.

"We haven't stayed up all night in ten years,"
Doctor Squires said to her.

"Yes we did."

"We did?"

"We did. New Year's Eve, four years ago.
Remember we found that coke that you hid from the
eighties? You said that made it vintage. So we did it
and then we made love on the terrace covered in
these giant blankets – and we woke up Steph and you
told her we were out there trying to save a sick
pigeon?"

"I do remember that."

Doctor Squires laughed. And then he sighed.

"What happened to us, Kristen?"

Mrs Squires looked at him. "You're kidding, right?"

"Yeah. I'm kidding," he said, standing up.

"Where are you going?" Mrs Squires asked him.

"To order another bottle of champagne."

She showed him the bottle. "We've barely started
this one yet."

"I know," Doctor Squires said. "I wanna see if I can
fire the cork into the hotel pool next time."

She followed him back inside.

It was like he was blessing her with his cock. He fucked
her in the head, the cunt and then came over each of
her breasts. His balls were empty now and his dick was
twitching like a dying man, but even this wasn't the
end of it. Not as far as she was concerned. She put
each of her long breasts up to her mouth and sucked
the white semen off each of her dark nipples – as if she
were her own starving baby – while the rest of the cum

on her tits ended up all over her mouth and chin. She dribbled like Dracula.

It had been a long time since Doctor and Mrs Squires had seen sex like this; the last time they came to this hotel, you could only get softcore pornography on cable.

And the time before that, they hadn't needed pornography at all in order to have sex...

Mrs Squires sat at the foot of the bed – on Doctor Squires's cock – naked and sweating, concentrating on the screen like it was her *Cindy Crawford Shape Your Body Workout*... While Doctor Squires held on to his wife by his fingertips – blindly rubbing her clitoris – as he looked over her shoulder; staring at the light that came from the television like he was trying to bring on a sneeze.

Twenty minutes later, they were still sitting at the foot of the bed – only now they were side by side. Doctor Squires turned to his wife.

"So how was it for you?" he asked.

"Not much story."

"I was talking about our sex."

"I know you were, Jeffrey... Have we got any more of those pills I like. I don't know what they are, but they're fuckin' fabulous."

Doctor Squires reached down and picked up a discarded bathrobe. He went inside a pocket and took out a bottle of pills. He gave it a shake.

Mrs Squires smiled like a baby as she heard the rattle … and just for a second, their fingers intertwined as the bottle was passed.

"I want a divorce," Doctor Squires said.

"Me too."

twenty-nine

"So...um..."

"I'll call you this week, Shapiro."

"This week? When?"

"Some time during the week...I'm going to be really busy. At work."

"The world needs copies, huh?"

"Something like that."

"Well...cool."

"Bye."

"Peace."

"Ow. Don't hug too tight, Shapiro. Sunburn."

"Right. Bye."

All the way back to his apartment, Luke was replaying what they'd just said on the steps of Stephanie's penthouse. He remembered the last time they'd said good-bye there. They'd kissed so passionately he'd felt her leg curl backward. If she did that now, Luke would only wonder if she was checking if she'd stood in dog shit. The old paranoia was back.

"So…um…"

"I'll call you this week, Shapiro."

"This week? When?"

"Some time during the week…"

Perhaps this loop would have gone on all night had it not been snapped when he opened the front door of his apartment. He knew straight away that something was wrong. No one was screaming. He put down his boombox and then dropped his duffel bag in the hall, hoping the noise would illicit some response. Nothing.

"Dad? Mom?" he called out.

He tried the living room… Then his parents' bedroom. There was no one there either. But as he approached the bathroom, he heard muffled cries.

"Mom?"

"I'm fine, honey. It's okay," she said.

Luke opened the door a crack. His mom was sitting on the edge of the bath, crying.

"Please, Luke," she told him. "Please leave."

"Didn't you hear me calling you?"

"I didn't want you to see me like this."

Luke knew this wasn't true. He'd seen her cry a million times. She just didn't want to tell him the reason why she was crying tonight. He went and sat down next to her.

"Mom, tell me what's happened," he said, putting his arm around her.

"I can't be poor, Luke...I don't know how to do it."

She started to sob with all the frustration of a child. Unable to speak, she pointed to a pill bottle on the counter. Luke looked at the label. It was Valium. He filled a glass of water and handed it to her with one of the pills. His mom popped it.

"Now, Mom, tell me what happened. What did he do?"

"He...risked...everything," his mom said, like she was having to use an oxygen mask between each word. "Over...and...over...again."

"Mom, here, have another drink of water."

His mom took a shallow sip and a deep breath. She tried again.

"He was chasing his losses...and now his losses are chasing him." She turned to her son. "I think they've caught him, Luke."

"Mom. Mom. It's gonna be fine."

"I'm so sorry, Luke. This isn't fair to you."

"It's cool. I can take it."

"You can. I know that...I just wanted it to be easy for you. And it's always so...fucking...hard."

"What?"

"Everything."

"It's gonna be fine, Mom. I talked to Dad. He said he was gonna fix it."

"I wish I could believe that, Luke. I wish I could believe in that fairy tale where the elves appear during

the night and fix everything for you...but when I get up in the morning, there's only the usual trail of carpet slugs by the porch."

"Mom. It's gonna be fine."

"Okay, sweetie. Okay. I'm sorry...I'll be alright."

"You sure?"

"I'm sure. You don't have to worry about me."

Luke kicked a box of walkmen as he went up to his room. Why did his dad always have to do things like this – things where, if they went wrong, he would never speak of them again? But if they went right, he would never shut up about them? Why did it always have to be at the extremities? Did he think this was the American way?

There was only one way this was going to be sorted out.

As soon as he got into his room, he gave the finger to the bedroom window (to wherever his dad might have been in New York that night). Then he looked inside his mini-fridge at his bricks of weed. Then he checked his pager, which was buzzing on his desk over and over again.

Then he collapsed onto the bed, face down into his pillow.

He couldn't do this any more. Not on top of how he was feeling about Stephanie. Instinctively, he did what he always did in times of stress. He pressed play on his boombox. He immediately pressed stop. That was only going to make him think of Stephanie more. He turned on the radio instead – just as "Memory Lane (Sittin' in da Park)" by Nas was beginning.

He sobbed as deeply and loudly as his mom had downstairs. It was like they were watching the same sad movie in different rooms.

thirty

"Hey. It's Steph. Leave a message."

"Yo. Steph. Hey. It's me, Luke. I know you said
you'd call me this week, and it's a week from when you
said that...so, well, I guess there's still time in the
week, really...Technically, there's still a few hours left.
I hope you're aware of that...Listen, are you not
calling me back cuz I said I love you? Cuz that's stupid.
I mean, I didn't mean it really...And even if I did, I'm
going to college in three weeks so it's not like it
matters. You know what? Fuck it. I meant it. I do love
you. I'm not scared to say it. I fucking love you and if
that scares you, well, then...then...*Jesus! Steph!* All I
did was tell you that I loved you in the shower. You're
acting like it's something out of *Psycho*; like you need
to cut me out like cancer before I start sticking to you
like shit to a security blanket. Well, if that's what you
think, then fuck you. You know what? Fuck off. You're
a bitch. Good-bye."

Doctor Squires was staring at the signatures at the bottom of his certificates in his office. All the years he'd spent in here, and he'd never realized his walls had been tagged.

There was a knock at the door.

"Come in," he said.

He heard the door open and a familiar voice said, "Hey."

Doctor Squires turned round. "Shapiro?"

Luke was staring down at his sneakers. "You were right," he said. "She got bored."

Doctor Squires shook his head. "It's not a question of being right, son. It's a question of being old. In time you'll see that's just the way it is in a relationship: you're either awed or bored. And whichever one you are, chances are the other person's the other... What did she actually say?"

"She said that she always saw the dopeness, and I always saw the wackness."

Doctor Squires looked at him.

Luke explained. "You know, it's like that stuff about the glass being either half full or half empty."

"And what if there's a deposit on the bottle, Shapiro? Now who's the pessimist?"

Doctor Squires saw the faintest flicker of a smile on Luke's face.

"You are who you are, Lucas."

Luke nodded sadly.

"What else did she say?" Doctor Squires asked him.

"Nothing."

"Uh-huh."

"Not after I told her I loved her."

"With all due respect to my stepdaughter, Luke – fuck her. Fuck 'em all… It's like Biggie says, 'bitches I like 'em brainless…'"

"'Guns I like 'em stainless steel.'"

They stared in silence for a while, listening to the music in their heads.

"So. You couldn't save your marriage, huh?" Luke asked him.

"Turns out it wasn't worth saving."

"That's too bad."

Doctor Squires shrugged sadly. "We are orphaned many years before our parents die, Luke. And we are divorced long before our spouses leave. Do you understand?"

"I think so… And you remember that other thing you once told me? That stuff about men doing the things they needed to do to become the men they need to become… or something?"

"Not really."

"Well, I need your help."

"What is it, Luke?"

"Do you know anyone who could maybe use some weed? I have a little extra weight to unload this month."

Doctor Squires mentally flitted through the case notes of his clients, matching their various mental conditions with their medicines. He couldn't think of anyone who couldn't use some weed.

"We could probably work something out, Luke."

thirty-one

"Thanks for letting me come with you, Luke. I feel this is a big step in our relationship."

The doors pinged to reveal the men and their Uzis.

"You're welcome, Doctor Squires," Luke said, walking confidently out of the elevator. "Hey, fellas. Lookin' good today. This is Doctor... *Doctor Squires?*"

Luke turned round. Doctor Squires was still inside the elevator with his back against its wall. His fingers were spread like starfish.

Luke went back and walked him out.

"It's okay, Doctor Squires."

"Uh-huh."

"Really. You'll be fine. Just don't be yourself."

Doctor Squires had been doing a bad impression of himself for such a long time now that he frequently wondered who he was meant to be. It was easier to act like Luke. He could see the difference that came of Luke being in a world that he understood. (Parents and girls? He was begging for drugs and contemplating putting a gun to his head…Drugs and guns? He was John Travolta walking down the street with a can of paint.)

Percy appeared at the end of the hallway. Luke could see the chunky plastic handle of a Glock pistol sticking out from above his pants. "Who da *fuck* are you?" he snarled.

Doctor Squires looked at him. "Who the *fuck* are you?"

"He's with me, Percy," Luke said quickly. "He's cool."

"I'm cool, Percy," Doctor Squires said.

"I'll be da judge of dat."

Percy signaled for them to follow him, but again Luke had to go back for Doctor Squires. This time he was standing right in front of one of the Uzi guys, staring him out.

"Stop that," the Uzi guy told him.

Doctor Squires blinked. "Sorry."

"The drowning represents your inability to get a handle on your life, what you're doing, perhaps your business," Doctor Squires said. "And the girl – well, I don't know. When in doubt, I usually go with your mother."

"My mom?" Percy said, handing Doctor Squires the spliff. "Now you say dat, it makes a lot more sense to me. You see, my mom doesn't approve of what I do. She sees dat *Cosby Show* on TV and she tinks dis America is da land of opportunity for black people."

Doctor Squires shook his head. "There are no role models for black people, Percy. Such people only make it *harder* for others to succeed – because the white establishment will only allow a few black people to get through."

"Man, dat's da truth."

"Race is the challenge by which God tests us, Percy."

They gave each other a fist pound.

Luke unfolded his arms. "Listen, guys… I hate to interrupt, but, Percy, I need more…"

"But da ting is, da dream is different every time," Percy said to Doctor Squires. "What's does it mean when people have recurring dreams?"

Doctor Squires shrugged. "That they lack imagination."

Many years ago, Doctor Squires had a recurring dream that he was in bed with another man. This other man wasn't doing anything (he was asleep), but he was naked – as was Doctor Squires. So Doctor Squires tried to move away from him, but no matter how far he tried to move, he could still feel some part of this other man's body touching him. He was getting more and more agitated. Until finally, he woke himself up and he realized the naked body he could feel was that of his first wife. And he was only slightly relieved.

Luke tried again. "So, like I wuz sayin', Percy. I need more drugs."

"How much more does Lukey need?"

"Another ten ounces."

"How you gwana unload an extra ten ounces dis week, boy?"

"I've been able to expand my client roster. I've had a few referrals from another practice."

Percy looked across at Doctor Squires.

"So what's dis Freud say I wanna do to my mother...?"

thirty-two

"So every man wanna kill his father and fuck his mother...? Hooo-boy. I tink dis Freud is half right. Plenty of times I coulda strangled my mother as well."

"Please, Doctor Squires, that's the third time you've said that."

"I can't help it, Luke, I love the way that Percy speaks. It's so cool."

"But you don't even sound like him."

How could he? Doctor Squires thought. Black people were cool. He thought it might have something to do with their hair. There wasn't a lot you could do with it – so there wasn't a lot you could do wrong with it. A black man has never had a mullet.

"I wanna be cool, Luke," Doctor Squires told him.

"Is that why you've got the trilby hat on?"

"Doesn't it look a bit cool?"

Luke looked at him.

"Actually, it kinda does," he said.

Doctor Squires smiled and pressed play on the boombox. "Cab Fare" by Souls of Mischief kicked in. "So where we gonna push the cart to first?" he asked.

Luke pressed stop.

"Right, Doctor Squires, if we're gonna do this, we're gonna do it right. You gotta be a little more careful."

"Don't worry, Luke. I'm not going back to prison."

"Good. Let's establish a few ground rules. Number one: we use pagers. Someone pages us, and we call them back from a payphone. We never use home phones for this type of stuff. Never."

"That's great, Luke. I already have a pager for my medical practice."

"Number two: we sell weed by the gram, by the eighth, and by the ounce. Gram's the highest profit margin but it's also the most potent. That's why we try to encourage people to buy the grams."

Doctor Squires nodded.

"Number three: you make half of all sales on any clients you refer…"

"Oh, don't worry about that, Luke."

"What do you mean?"

"I don't need the money."

"Wait…so why are you doing this?"

"You know, for fun…But, just out of interest, exactly how much money are we trying to make here?"

"As much as possible…"

"And what's all this for, Luke? If you don't mind my asking?"

"I gotta help my family, Doctor Squires… And I gotta help myself. I might have given up on life, you see, but it's just as expensive for a miserable man to live as a happy one."

Doctor Squires pressed play on the boombox.

"We deal together, Luke. We deal together."

"Look, Principal Edwards," Luke said. "I can give you two grams for a hundred and twenty-five dollars. Anything less than that, I don't make a profit."

The principal frowned and went back to eating his sandwich without a plate, eating the breadcrumbs off his chest like a bird.

"Please, Luke…" Doctor Squires said to him. "Do you know how much teachers make?"

Luke shot Doctor Squires a look. This wasn't one of his referrals. Besides, this apartment looked alright to him.

"People don't go into teaching for the money, Luke," Doctor Squires continued. "It's a vocation."

"Actually, it was for the vacations," the principal told him. "And the early finish. Teaching's basically the graduate equivalent of being a garbageman."

"But the kids," Doctor Squires said. "Surely, they make it all…"

"Don't you believe it. They say hell is other people? It's other people's kids. I thought that it would at least be easier teaching in an elementary school, before puberty kicked in. I mean, it made sense, right? To tackle the Wolfman before the full moon, rather than after it? But in the end, it made very little difference. And every year they get worse."

"Well, I guess I can't argue with you about that," Doctor Squires said, sitting down. "The other day this kid in the street – he couldn't have been more than eight years old – he called me a 'Motherfucker.' Can you believe that?"

The principal shrugged. "What are we going to do?"

Yeah. That was exactly what Luke was thinking. "So what's it gonna be, Principal Edwards?" he asked him. "Whichever way I put in the numbers, I can't do it for any less than one hundred and twenty-five dollars…"

"You always were very good at math, Luke…And English too as I remember." He turned again to Doctor Squires. "Do you know I was once teaching this boy that if you added the suffix 'ly' to an adjective, you often had an adverb. And the next day he told me that if you added the word 'head' to a one syllable curse word, you often had an insult. And he was right."

Luke looked at him. "You remember that?"

The principal nodded.

"And it still makes you smile, doesn't it?" Doctor Squires said to him.

He nodded again. "Okay, Luke, you got yourself a deal."

Luke was looking at the old folk milling around by the zoo in Central Park. Everyone else was wearing as little as possible as the heat wave continued. It was too hot for shame. People offered their imperfect bodies to the sun like the infirm exposing themselves to a shrine; hoping by some miracle that they might just feel a little cooler. But if old people still needed to wear so many clothes when it was as hot as this, Luke wondered if this was why so many of these poor old dears perished during the winter in New York – they were crushed by the weight of their own clothes.

"Here he comes," Doctor Squires said, pointing out a bearded old man. "That's Oliver."

Luke blinked. "Man, he's even wearing more clothes than the rest of them."

Doctor Squires smiled at the irony of this statement. He'd originally started treating Oliver because of his refusal to wear clothes – he was convinced that the government had hidden almost invisible listening devices in everybody's garments. (Doctor Squires didn't normally make home visits, but Oliver's poor wife begged him. She was at the end of her tether, having to spend her retirement looking at a naked old man.) It was a long process, but eventually they made a breakthrough. Oliver agreed to wear shoes. Although sometimes Doctor Squires wondered whether this was, in fact, a step back: Oliver looked even more ridiculous being naked *except* for his shoes. (And there was undoubtedly something tragic in not being able to tie your laces without smelling your ass.) But, little by little, garment by garment, they had managed to get to where they were today: vague overdressing.

Doctor Squires held out his hand. "Oliver! How's the golf game?"

"Not bad, Doc. Not bad."

"And your wife?"

"Still having flashbacks."

"I'm sorry to hear that. Call my office to make an appointment... Now, how much marijuana can I get you?"

"An eighth."

"I don't suppose we coulda just left the cart downstairs, could we, Luke?"

"Not today."

"But I can't believe it's a fifth floor walkup..."

"Please, Doctor Squires. Behave. This is my connection."

"But who the fuck lives in a fifth floor..."

"Hi, Luke!" Eleanor said, opening her door.

"...walkup. *Hello*," Doctor Squires said, removing his hat.

"I'm Eleanor," she said.

"I'm, uh, Hayden."

"You don't have to use an alias with her, Doctor Squires."

"Oh. Well then, I'm Jeff."

"And I'm still Eleanor... Come on in."

She turned and went into her apartment.

"Doctor Squires," Luke whispered, as they followed her. "You're crushing your hat..."

"I can't believe you've carried your cart up all those flights of stairs," Eleanor said, as they walked into her living room.

"It was nothing," Doctor Squires told her.

Luke rolled his eyes. "Well, the thing is, Eleanor, I got a nasty feeling there could've been some of Giuliani's men down on the street."

Eleanor's eyes narrowed. "Fucking Giuliani...! Thinks he can clean up the city. He doesn't know Jack shit. He still calls him Mr Shit."

Doctor Squires audibly sighed.

"So... how much you want?" Luke asked her.

"A quarter," Eleanor told him. "I'm going to New Hampshire to meet that guy. The fucker. So, I'm... you know... just, packing..."

"He doesn't appreciate you," Doctor Squires said.

Eleanor smiled. "How'd you guess?" she asked him.

"He couldn't possibly."

She studied his face. "That's a compliment, right?"

Doctor Squires nodded.

"Let me find my purse," she said.

She eventually found it under her cat.

"He was hiding it on purpose," Eleanor said. "My neighbor will be looking after him, but he doesn't want me to go. You can see it by that far off look in his eyes, can't you?"

Luke thought that cats always have that far off, distracted look – like they've placed a bet.

"I can see it," Doctor Squires told her.

Eleanor handed Luke his money – along with her CD.

"Thanks," Luke said. "Greatest Hits?"

Eleanor shrugged. "It's really only three songs and a lot of remixes. It's actually kind of more like one song."

Doctor Squires looked at the picture on the cover.

"You were in Emergency Breakthrough?" he asked her.

Eleanor nodded coyly.

"No shit! I loved your music."

"No shit!" Eleanor said, losing all composure. "See, Luke? See? I'm not just making this stuff up." She turned to Doctor Squires. "I'm trying to educate him. Show him there's a whole world beyond rap music."

"Me too," Doctor Squires told her. "I want him to know that there's more to the seventies than just fat collars, slim microphones and bad impressions of Twiki."

"Who?" Luke asked him.

"Never mind," Doctor Squires told him. "You should just listen to what this woman tells you. She's as smart and talented as she is beautiful."

Eleanor's chin dimpled. "Awww," she said, turning to Luke. "He's crazy, right?"

"A total lunatic," Luke said.

Luke and Doctor Squires pushed the cart down the street. It was getting dark now.

"You know it's funny," Doctor Squires said. "You came to me and told me you have no friends, but I look at the people you meet through your job, and I see you have friends."

Luke shook his head. "I'm not their friend, Doctor Squires. To them, I'm just their dope dealer."

"But I see the way they act with you."

"They're clients. It's not the same thing."

"You are my client, Luke. And I am yours. And we are friends. It can be the same thing…In fact, the more I think about it, the more I think we do the same thing – except you're giving people the real shit. I just give them chemicals. I prescribe lies."

Doctor Squires knew it wasn't always like that – but it was now. He could barely listen to their problems, so nothing improved. Not even his doodling. (He wondered why that was: you could doodle your whole life and it didn't get any better.)

"I want to do this, Luke," Doctor Squires told him.

"Do what?"

"What you do. Exactly what you do. With a cart and a boombox and a hip hop mixtape. It's been such a long time since a form of musical expression was so raw, so real. It's like therapy, really. Except doper. Of course, I'd like to occasionally throw some other stuff into the mix – 'All the Young Dudes' by Mott the Hoople, perhaps – but you'll need someone to follow in your footsteps. When you're gone."

Luke looked at him. "Are you okay, Doctor Squires?"

"I'm fine, Luke. Totally fine. I'm just… unfulfilled."

"Well, this isn't for you."

"But it's for you?"

thirty-three

Back in the day, when Doctor Squires still listened to his patients' problems, he had come to the conclusion that, for most men, being married was like clinical depression: it felt worst first thing in the morning. A man would wake up with an erection – having spent the night dreaming about fucking whoever he wanted – and it was hard for him not to resent his wife, just a little bit. But as the day wore on, and he had to deal with reality – going to work; paying bills; worrying about losing his hair – he would be grateful to be part of a team; to have someone to fall back on. So his mood would naturally lighten...

But right now, Doctor Squires completely denied that his feelings toward his own marriage could possibly be subject to fluctuation.

"No, Kristen, please don't go!"

"It's the shock at seeing the suitcase," Mrs Squires told him, as she stood in the hall. "You'll feel differently once I'm gone."

"No I won't. I love you."

"No you don't, Jeffrey – you just think you do."

"What difference does it make, if it feels the same…? Can't we at least try again? We used to have so much in common."

"We shared the same temptations. That's not the same thing either."

"But…"

"Look, Jeffrey, I don't wanna have to hide my true feelings any more – finding sanctuary in early nights; silently screaming as I pull a jersey over my head. Do you think that I like spending hours in the bath? It's the only room with a lock on the door."

"And you think that leaving will make you happy?"

"I don't know if I'll ever be happy – but this isn't the bad relationship I want to be in."

"Please, Kristen, don't leave me all alone. I can't be all alone."

One blink now and his tears would drop.

Mrs Squires looked away. "Please, Jeffrey, don't do this."

"Lonely old men were cruel young men. Is this what I deserve? Was I ever cruel?"

Mrs Squires was silent.

"Please, Kristen, you're wrong about how you think I feel about you. I couldn't possibly love you any more!"

She picked up her suitcase. "Neither can I."

Doctor Squires was about to drop to his knees and beg her to stay when he heard a noise behind him. He turned round. Stephanie was standing outside her room.

"Are you leaving too?" he asked her.

"She's staying for the next few weeks, Jeffrey. We'll deal with all the details when I return from rehab."

"Details...?" Doctor Squires asked. He turned to Stephanie. "Please. Say something to your mother, Steph."

"Leave her out of this, Jeffrey." She turned to Stephanie, too. "Sweetheart, go back into your room."

Stephanie's eyes flitted between them like small, panicky steps.

She went back into her room, sat down on her bed and contemplated her future...but the irrational question in her head took her right back to the time when her mom first told her that she was going to be marrying Doctor Squires: would she have to get used to a new name? Only the flashing light on her answering machine managed to pull her gaze away from the floor. She played back the message from the call she'd just missed.

"Hey Steph. It's Luke...so, I guess you're ignoring me, huh? That's a shame cuz it'd be nice to hang out or whatever before I go to school. The school year is rapidly approaching, as you know and, well, I miss you. Call me back."

Her phone rang again. She picked it up quickly. "Shapiro?"

"Huh?"

"Justin?"

"Why you callin' me Shapiro?"

"No reason ... how was Florence?"

"Seville."

"Right. How was it?"

"Crazy, yo. Mad crazy. I'll tell you all about it. We're gonna hit this club downtown tonight. Wanna come?"

"Totally."

thirty-four

Luke's mom was sitting on the curb smoking a cigarette, next to a fire hydrant, next to a removal truck. Luke abandoned his cart and sprinted toward her.

"Mom! Mom! What happened?"

His mom looked up at him, squinting at the sun.

"I'll give you three guesses," she said.

His dad and two removal men were walking down the steps that led from their apartment to the street. The removal men were carrying their grandfather clock on its side. His dad was chaperoning them.

"Please be careful with that," his dad said to them. "That was a wedding present from my parents."

Luke ran up to him.

"Dad. Wait! I have money. I have money." He turned to the removal men. "Put that down! I have the money."

"Luke, stop," his dad told him.

"Would you please listen to me, Dad? I have twenty-six thousand dollars. That should be more than enough."

He waited for his dad to say something, but he just carried on walking with the removal men.

Luke should have known that his dad would have reacted like this; that he'd never believe that a kid could make that much money. Let alone a kid like Luke.

"Dad, it's true," Luke told him. "Twenty-six thousand dollars."

His dad stopped and looked at him. "Oh, Luke..."

"Yes?"

"It's not enough, Luke. Not even close."

Luke suddenly recalled all those endless brown envelopes that had been delivered to their apartment over the years. He remembered thinking that bills were like cassettes. Each had a plastic window. Each told you how long you had left...Except he realized now you couldn't always just flip the tape over and start again. *Twenty six thousand dollars and it wasn't even close.* This was the silent "b" in debt: there was always a sting in the tail, and you never saw it coming.

"You said you'd fix it, Dad. You said you'd fix it."

"Lucas, I'm going to need you to go upstairs and pack your stuff. There are plenty of cardboard boxes; the walkmen aren't moving."

"That's all you've got to say to me...? *Unbefuckinglievable.*"

"Luke, do you have to swear all the time?"

Luke stared at him. Their lives were going down the toilet; they'd been thrown out onto the street – and his dad wanted him to choose a better adjective. There wasn't one. Not one that you could put inside another word; not one that could better describe a situation so screwed up that they'd been literally fucked from the inside out.

"Dad. How did you let it get to this?"

His dad turned to his son and looked him up and down.

"Grow up, Luke."

Luke could feel the middle finger of his right hand begin to extend – just as it had all those times that he'd flipped his dad the bird from behind his closed bedroom door. But what good had it done? Had it really made Luke feel better? It had certainly never made his dad feel worse.

And it wouldn't do now, either.

His dad was fuck knows how many tens of thousands of dollars in debt – and Luke thought that a bit of sign language for "Stick it up your ass" was going to mortally wound him? It wouldn't even touch the sides.

Luke's finger retracted.

To leave only a fist.

He pulled it back and got ready to let go.

His dad caught sight of him in his peripheral vision, but he never turned his attention from the removal men in the truck.

"I asked you to grow up, Luke," he said. "But not like that... *Gentlemen. Please.* Easy with the grandfather clock. It's very important to us."

His dad sighed and walked toward the truck... and Luke let his arm drop down to his side again. The situation was all too ridiculous for words. Or sign-language. Or fists. The grandfather clock said it all. It had been showing twenty past two for as long as Luke could remember. He went to sit down on the curb next to his mom.

He looked at her cigarette.

"You got another?"

"You smoke?" she asked him.

"Everything."

And they smoked together, watching as the grandfather clock – which had refused to chime of its own accord in all those years in their apartment – was walked into a tight space in the back of the truck, clanging with every step. It was too late now.

thirty-five

"Do you remember when we gave you this grandfather clock as a wedding present, Andy?"

"Yes, Pop."

"Can you remember what I said?"

"Uh-huh."

"Well?"

"Uh…"

"Come on, son. Speak up."

"You said, 'Now make me a grandfather'…"

"That's right, I did…and you did. You gave us Luke."

Luke's grandfather smiled and squeezed Luke's cheek, but the smile vanished as he turned back to his son. "I just never thought we'd get the clock back as well…"

Luke's grandfather looked over it again. "Nice to see you've kept it in such good upkeep," he said, sarcastically. "When did it stop working, Andy?"

"Twenty past two," he told him.

Luke's mom quickly covered her mouth to cover her smile.

"Our son has a sense of humor," Luke's grandfather said, turning to his wife. "He has nowhere to live, but he has a sense of humor...I'm off to watch the Mets on TV. If I set off now, I might just make the ninth inning."

Luke watched his grandfather shuffle down the hallway – weaving his way through all their cardboard boxes – with one hand on a walking stick, and the other on his hip: old people's fencing.

Luke's mom turned to his grandmother. "Thanks for putting us up, Evelyn."

"It's the least we can do," she told her, taking her by the hand, "for having given birth to a son who can't keep a roof over his family's head...I just hope that second bedroom's big enough for all three of you."

Luke couldn't remember the last time he'd seen his grandparents, but he was sure their eyebrows weren't white then, and they didn't shake as much as they did now. It was like they'd just walked out of the deep freeze. Luke decided that there was nothing to be gained in getting older, but that was the same if you were seventy-seven or seventeen. For a split second, at the moment of our births, everyone held the distinction of once being the youngest person on the planet. How could you achieve anything as monumental as that ever again?

He turned over in his Z-bed to lie on his side, momentarily forgetting that he'd now be facing his parents, who were sleeping in the double bed. And to make matters worse, his eyes had acclimatized to the dark now. Luke couldn't remember the last time he'd seen his parents sleeping together, but he was sure he'd never seen them sleeping like this. He could see his dad nuzzle his mom as he slept. His mom made a little noise and pulled him to her. Luke wondered whether it was the uncertainty of the situation that was bringing them closer together. He could see the shapes of their bodies through the duvet; they looked like a pair of question marks, spooning like that... Or, maybe it was the realization that despite everything, they still had each other – and that perhaps, deep down, this was always the most important thing to them.

You take the life that you have from the life that you wanted, and the difference is your wackness.

Suddenly, Luke realized there was only one of two choices to make in life: review your desires, or change your circumstances.

thirty-six

Stephanie opened the front door to her penthouse and blinked.

"Shapiro?"

It was still early.

"Look, Steph, I know the summer's almost over, but I think we can make this work."

"Luke…"

"Hear me out. People do the long distance thing. And it's not like we're going to school so far from each other, you know? I mean, it's like a four hour train ride. We could alternate weekends…"

Luke heard a voice call out from behind her: "Shapiro?"

"Is that Justin?" Luke asked her.

She didn't have to answer. Justin appeared. He was shirtless and just waking up.

"Yo, Shapiro," he said. "Do you have any weed?"

Luke seemed to recoil and advance at the same time as repulsion toward Stephanie, and anger toward

Justin, overwhelmed him at once. And he stayed perfectly still.

"No," he said to Justin.

"Okay," Justin said, and he disappeared back into the penthouse.

The stare Luke gave Justin didn't change as it moved over to Stephanie.

"Luke…" she said.

"Where's Doctor Squires?" he asked her.

"He just left for Fire Island."

"With your mom?"

"No, she's in rehab."

"Peace."

Luke turned and walked to the elevator.

"Wait," Stephanie said.

Luke turned round.

Stephanie's mouth opened, but there weren't any words. It was as if she were struggling to find the right ones… Or as if she hadn't expected Luke to turn round. Either way, it took Luke right back to when he was sitting alone on the roof at the graduation party, when he could only imagine what moving silent mouths were saying about him in the form of a subtitle.

"It's for the best, Luke," she finally said.

Yeah. That was pretty much what Luke would have imagined.

The elevator arrived and Luke left.

thirty-seven

Doctor Squires was listening to "Ready to Die" on the hi-fi in his beach house, thinking back to that conversation he'd had with Kristen about his Catholic patient who killed himself. If to die for your beliefs was the ultimate act of faith, Doctor Squires decided, then suicide was the ultimate act of atheism. And even if there was a God, surely no one could ever be *completely* guilty of the sin of suicide. After all, if a person was a combination of his mind and body, then it could always be shown that a part of that person didn't want to die – it might be the grand flailing of limbs as they fought for air; or merely the subtle chain reaction of blood cells trying desperately to clot a gaping wound – but surely these mindless acts, however futile, had to count for something.

Then again, could you really argue a technicality with God?

Fuck it. He'd soon find out.

Besides, he was glad now that he had that conversation with Kristen. He could just imagine her

crying at his funeral, praying for his eternally damned soul at the altar. And the huge effigy of Christ would look down on her from his cross, with his crown of thorns and nails in his hands and feet. Kristen would look up – and all she would see would be his ribcage. And she'd think about how she should really be at home doing her *Cindy Crawford Shape Your Body Workout.*

Fucking hell! He was even more determined to do it now.

He checked that the suicide note he'd written was still fastened to Jesus Christ's collar (he was sleeping in the bedroom): "MY OWNER HAS KILLED HIMSELF. PLEASE TAKE CARE OF ME." Then he snorted a final long line of coke from the table. Except it wasn't really a line; it twisted between all the other drugs that covered the table, and Doctor Squires's head swam from side to side as he snorted it. He looked like a boxer loosening his neck before he entered the ring…And then Doctor Squires wandered around the beach house, twirling his rope like a cowboy, looking for a suitable rafter to lasso his head from…

There was a knock on the front door. He dropped the rope and went to answer it.

"Luke," he said. "How are you?"

"Shitty."

"Yeah. Dark Times."

"We got evicted."

"You're homeless now?"

"As good as."

Doctor Squires looked from side to side. "Well, don't let the mayor see you."

He grabbed Luke and pulled him inside.

"I apologize for the mess," Doctor Squires said. "I wasn't expecting company…"

"You've been doing all these drugs?" Luke asked him.

"It's an experiment. An experience. Life. Salvation. Drugs…Go ahead. Help yourself."

Luke looked at all the weed, powders, ampoules, and capsules that covered the table – and at all the dots and dashes of the round and easy to swallow tablets that covered any remaining space like Morse code.

"I haven't done most of this before, Doctor Squires," he told him.

"Come now, Lucas. Be a pal. Do it."

Five hours later, Luke's huge pupils were rolling around his eyeballs like marbles in a tin can. He wasn't entirely sure of what had gone on before. He could remember starting to take the drugs on the table in a logical manner…Unfortunately, it was the logic of a child. So, for example, the "purple haze" weed had been ingested along with a red pill and a blue pill – because that made purple, didn't it…?

And he could remember the end of the session: putting a pill into his mouth and water suddenly pouring all over his chin. ("That works best when you put the pill in your mouth, and *then* drink the water," Doctor Squires had told him.) Oh, and somewhere in between, they might have grilled a salmon and played Trivial Pursuit.

Now they were sitting on the beach, staring at the ocean.

"The ocean," Doctor Squires said. "This is all I need. Forget the city. The city is wrong. I just want to wrap myself in the ocean."

"I cannot speak."

"That's the spirit, Luke. Go with the flow. A mighty oak may fall, but the greatest storm has never pulled up a single blade of grass... Come on, hit me with it, ocean! Fucking hit me! You don't think I can take it? I can take everything you throw at me, fucking sea."

Doctor Squires put eye drops into each of his glassy bloodshot marbled eyes. Luke's eyes felt sore too. He motioned to Doctor Squires.

"You sure?" Doctor Squires asked him.

"Hm?"

"It's liquid acid."

Luke groaned.

A hot girl in a white tank top and a short skirt walked along the beach with a dog.

"Look at those tits," Doctor Squires said.

Luke had noticed that men always saw breasts like they were religious apparitions. They needed confirmation from other men that they'd seen them too. (In fact, they often felt the need to confirm it with the woman who was actually attached to the tits.) But on this occasion, Luke was grateful to know that this wasn't a hallucination.

"I want to...vagina," Luke said.

"You said it, Luke...I should have known as soon as she told me she didn't like dogs. There's certain people you just can't trust. You know, Luke?"

"Um..."

"Luke, listen to me. I may not always be here for you, so I have to get all this out, okay...? Never trust anyone who doesn't smoke pot. Or listen to Bob Dylan. Do you hear me? Never trust anyone who doesn't like the beach, Luke. And never, ever, trust anyone who says they don't like dogs – alert the authorities immediately. And sure as shit don't marry them."

"Okay. Okay."

Doctor Squires looked back out over the ocean.

"Nothing's okay, Luke. None of it is going to be okay. Everything is going to be terrible...I tried to kill myself today, Luke. Twice. I left a suicide note on Jesus Christ's collar."

Luke looked at him.

"I tried it once with pills," Doctor Squires told him. "Turns out I have a very high tolerance for those. And

once by hanging...Hanging is very hard, Luke. I mean, a *noose*, for God's sake! Do you know how difficult it is to work out how to tie a noose when you're depressed...? Even then, it wasn't the end of it...I guess my wife was right. I should have lost some weight. I was actually looking for a stronger rafter to use when you turned up. I was determined to go out swinging, but it's a very serious thing, Luke. Gravity."

"Doctor Squires, what are you talking about?"

Doctor Squires shook his head. "I don't know, Luke," he said. "I just...I'm done."

"What do you mean?"

He looked down. "I'm pathetic," he said, his voice becoming as soft as the sand. "And do you know what the worst thing about being pathetic is...? You're always the last to know."

"I'm pathetic too, Doctor Squires. We all are."

"But my wife has left me. And I've lost my stepdaughter. Have you ever noticed how much they look alike? It's like I'm losing each of them twice...And my patients. They've all had enough of me too. All those wasted years encouraging people to 'open up' and 'share their emotions.' There is only one thing a man needs to know, Luke: crying doesn't help. It will never make a man stop hurting you. Or a woman start loving you again."

"But, Doctor Squires..."

"I've just made a mess of everything, Luke."

"No, you haven't. I don't know about your wife and your patients, but Stephanie told me that she finds your behavior funny…"

Doctor Squires wished he could believe Luke. He really did. He'd always thought that for most people children served the same purpose as religion: it was comforting to believe that some part of them would live on when they died. This is why there were very few old people who were both childless *and* Godless. But there was no self-interest in his relationship with Stephanie. This was why he reminded everyone that she was his stepdaughter. It wasn't because it meant less to him. It was because it meant more.

"Well, thanks for trying to make me feel better, Luke," Doctor Squires said, standing up. "I appreciate it. But my mind's made up. This is it. Last call. And I'm glad you're here to see me off – and I don't want you to worry, Luke. I was concerned before about what was going to happen to me, but I'm sure this way I'll go to heaven. I'm wearing my Aqua Sox."

And he set off down the beach to the ocean.

"Where are you going?" Luke said.

"In there…I'm ready to die, Luke."

He entered the water.

"Stop fucking around, Doctor Squires," Luke told him, eventually managing to get to his feet.

"I'm a weird old guy, Luke. You said it yourself."

"I didn't mean it," Luke called out to him,

stumbling down the beach – one foot crossing the other, making footprints in the sand of someone who'd put their shoes on the wrong feet...By the time he'd made it to the water, Doctor Squires was waist deep.

"You're my friend, Doctor Squires," Luke called out to him. "Actually you're my best friend. So come back. For me."

"You're not worth it, Shapiro."

"So that was all bullshit, huh? All that stuff about embracing your pain, making it a part of you."

But Doctor Squires just kept walking. Luke was screaming now as he tried to be heard above the sound of the waves. And he was screaming now in panic.

"You can't do this, Jeff! You can't just give up. Life is fucking hard and it's filled with pain and whatnot, but we take the pain cuz there's great stuff too! And we move on because we have friends...because we help each other!"

Luke was up to his chest now, and the waves were crashing over him. Up ahead, he could see Doctor Squires was up to his neck and the sea was beginning to cover him...And Luke finally knew the difference between sadness and depression. But it was too late now. Doctor Squires was gone.

Luke stumbled onto the shore, dripping with the brine of the ocean and his tears. Jesus Christ had appeared and was yipping at the water, the white foam of the sea always a hair's breadth from his white front paws as he moved up and down the beach as each wave encroached and retreated. Luke could see he still had the note attached to his collar. He took a deep breath to try to call him over, but the only thing that came out of his mouth was all the sea water he'd swallowed.

"Hey, Puke Shapiro!"

Luke looked up. Doctor Squires was sitting with his legs crossed further up the beach. Jesus Christ ran up to him and jumped into his lap, nestling into the human cradle. Luke wiped the sea from his chin and the tears from his eyes as he approached him.

"That was really fucking cheesy, what you just said," Doctor Squires told him.

"The world has enough assholes, Doctor Squires. Don't be another one."

"Now you sound like me."

Luke smiled. And Doctor Squires removed the note from Jesus Christ's collar.

"Let's go to the city," he told Luke. "Fill my prescriptions."

"Sounds good."

thirty-eight

Back in the penthouse, Jesus Christ was once again sitting in Doctor Squires's lap. Except Doctor Squires was wearing a bathrobe now, and Jesus Christ had a towel over his head. (They'd both been freshly showered.)

Luke handed over the bag full of pill bottles.

"Thank you, Luke," Doctor Squires said, placing it on the couch beside him.

"How you feeling?" Luke asked.

Doctor Squires shrugged.

"Don't do that again, please," Luke said to him. "You scared me."

"I'm sorry."

"Look, Doctor Squires…I have to get back. To my folks."

"So where exactly are you living now, Luke?"

"We're lodging with my grandparents. In New Jersey."

"I'm sorry to hear that."

"Yeah, well. I'm sorry to live it… You know, I never thought my family would be so destitute that we'd have to share a bedroom together. I could almost laugh about it."

"You should do, Luke. It's good for the poor to laugh. It annoys the rich."

"I'll try to remember that."

"And Luke – I'm sorry about Stephanie too… She would have been a lucky girl."

Luke looked down and nodded sadly.

"Well, I gotta go, Doctor Squires," he said. "My roomies will be wondering where I am."

"Good luck in school, Lucas. Try and fuck a black girl – I never got the chance to do that in college."

Luke smiled.

"Baby steps, Doctor Squires," he told him. "You'll be okay."

"I can't answer that."

"It wasn't a question… Peace, Jeff."

"Peace out, Luke."

He turned to go.

"Oh, Luke, I almost forgot…"

Doctor Squires pulled out a cassette from the pocket of his bathrobe and tossed it over to him.

"It's a mixtape, Luke. I made it for you."

He'd just pressed the button for the elevator when he heard the Squires's front door open again.

"Luke."

He turned round.

"Hi, Steph."

"Look, Luke, I'm sorry. It's…"

"Do me a favor, Steph – don't say nothin', okay? Just stand there until I leave. Let me look at you… I want to remember this. You see, I've never done it before."

"Done what?"

"Had my heart broken."

Luke stared into Stephanie's eyes and he recalled all the time they'd spent together that summer: the stolen conversation at the graduation party; strolling along the beautiful East Village street; their first kiss at the Lower Pond; standing in the twilight on the steps outside her home; pushing her through the Park on his cart. Fire Island… And he realized – the same thing that helped you was the same thing that hurt you. It was all in the past.

The elevator doors opened.

"Thanks, Steph," Luke said. "Take care of yourself."

He turned away from her and stepped inside.

"You too, Shapiro," Stephanie said, looking at him right until the doors closed.

By the time the elevator doors had opened again, on the ground floor, Luke had his headphones at the ready – and he pressed play on his walkman precisely as he walked out of the lobby and down onto the street. The first track on Doctor Squires's mixtape kicked in: "All the Young Dudes" by Mott the Hoople. Luke smiled and looked up at the terrace...just managing to avoid a descending water bomb which splattered all over the sidewalk.

thirty-nine

"Mom, you know I don't like meatloaf."

"In your house, you can set the menu, Andy...Oh, I'm sorry – you don't have a house, Mr Bigshot! Meatloaf's what we're eating."

"You love your mother's meatloaf," Luke's grandfather told him.

Luke's dad shook his head.

"Yes you do," his father told him again.

Luke's mom smiled at her husband reassuringly, and squeezed him by the hand.

"Can I have some more Dr Pepper, Evelyn?" Luke's grandfather asked his wife.

She poured some into his glass.

"Can I have some more Dr Pepper, Mom?" Luke's dad asked her.

She ignored him.

Luke's grandfather raised his glass.

"To your success, Luke... To the college man."

They all touched glasses and drank. (Luke's dad watched them.)

"So. What's next, Luke?" his grandfather asked him.

"Well … I'm off to college, I guess."

"And then?"

"And … then?"

"Your career, Luke," his grandmother asked him. "What are you going to do?"

"From what I can see, Grandma, it doesn't really make much difference. They all seem kind of the same."

"Nothing could be further from the truth, Luke," his dad told him.

"You're right, Dad." Luke turned to his grandfather. "I'm thinking about getting into music."

"This is the first I've heard of that," Luke's mom said.

"There's not much money in music," Luke's dad told him.

"Unless you're that Michael Jackson," his grandfather said.

Luke shrugged. "Well, I've always had an interest in English – alliteration, suffixes, and whatnot. Perhaps I could do a PhD in classical English literature …"

"And what will that entitle you to do, Lucas?" his grandfather asked. "Sign on for welfare with a quill?"

"What happened to math, Luke?" his grandmother asked him. "You used to love math."

"Luke's exceptional at math," Luke's dad told them.

"Yes," Luke said. "Yes, I am... I'm thinking about becoming a mathematician... Or a banker."

His grandparents nodded to each other.

"I mean, a fireman."

His grandfather looked baffled.

"A midwife!" Luke said.

"Lucas, stop confusing your grandparents," his mom told him.

"Actually, I was sort of thinking about becoming a shrink," Luke said.

His grandfather nodded. "It's a very interesting field, psychology..."

"Well, I figure I'm already an expert," Luke told them. "Cuz everyone around me is so fucking crazy."

It became so silent you could hear a bubble in a Dr Pepper pop... Then Luke's grandfather burst out laughing. Full blown laughing. Laughter that escalated like a fat man rolling down a hill. And it was this reaction that made everybody else join in. Including Luke. Despite everything he was feeling, he just couldn't help himself. Seeing his grandfather laughing so much like that: shaking on top of his shaking. He looked exactly like Jesus Christ drying himself.

forty

Doctor Squires was staring at the tags that covered his half-empty living room. They were on the coffee table, the couch, the lampstands. He recalled how Stephanie had walked in and asked him what he was doing. He told her he was marking his territory. She looked at him for a long time, and then asked if he needed any help. He'd smiled and handed her a Sharpie – and told her to also put her own tag on anything that she wanted... He'd looked at the one thing she'd chosen – an ornate mirror – and examined her tag. It was very similar to his own, except the "Squires" had been written in upper case and underlined several times. Stephanie had smiled at him, and he understood what his stepdaughter was saying.

Looking back, Doctor Squires conceded he'd probably gone too far with the tagging: he'd tagged a water bomb and received a warning from one of Giuliani's men... and now he was bored out of his

mind. And alone. (Yesterday, he'd burped into an empty coffee cup, just to hear the echo.)

Doctor Squires picked up the phone and dialed.

"Hello?" a woman said.

"Someone paged me from this number," Doctor Squires told her.

"Hi, Jeff. Um, this is Eleanor. Listen, I'm sorry to bother you, but Luke gave me your number. He said I should page you. I hope it's okay."

"It's okay. Yes."

"Well, listen, I was thinking, it's such a beautiful fall day…"

"It is, isn't it?"

"So, I was wondering whether you, um, fancied meeting up…for a coffee?"

Doctor Squires smiled. "Sounds good."